His mouth descended on hers in a hard, punishing kiss . . .

Sharon tried to escape the embrace, but she was no match for Nat's strength. She went limp in his arms . . . His kiss became tender, teasing her mouth until her lips parted in response. The kiss deepened, and Sharon found herself floating on a cloud of feeling.

Her body became fluid . . . she was molded to him, and her arms crept up around his neck of their own volition. Everything had ceased to exist except a sea of exquisite sensation.

"That's better," he said softly. "I knew I could change your opinion of me if I tried . . ."

Bantam Circle of Love Romances
Ask your bookseller for the books you have missed

1 GOLD IN HER HAIR by Anne Neville
2 ROYAL WEDDING by Mary Christopher
3 GATES OF THE SUN by Lucinda Day
4 DESIGN FOR ENCHANTMENT
 by Rachel Murray
5 THE CINDERELLA SEASON
 by Elaine Daniel
6 ASHTON'S FOLLY by Jean Innes
7 A RING AT THE READY by Anna West
8 THE RELUCTANT DAWN
 by Juliet Lawrence
9 THE HEATHER IS WINDBLOWN
 by Anne Saunders
10 VOICES OF LOVING by Anne Neville
11 MIDSUMMER DREAMS by Amalia James
12 LOVE'S DREAM by Christine Baker
13 THREAD OF SCARLET by Rachel Murray
14 THE BOTTICELLI MAN
 by Alexandra Blakelee
15 HERON'S KEEP by Samantha Clare

Dear Friend,

Enter the Circle of Love—and travel to faraway places with romantic heroes . . .

We read hundreds of novels and each month select the very best—from the finest writers around the world—to bring you these wonderful love stories . . . stories that let *you* share in a variety of beautiful romantic experiences.

With Circle of Love Romances, you treat yourself to a romantic holiday—anytime, anywhere. And because we want to please you, won't you write and let us know your comments and suggestions?

Meanwhile, welcome to the Circle of Love— we don't think you'll ever want to leave!

Best,

Cathy Camhy
Editor

CIRCLE OF LOVE™

Love's Dream

Christine Baker

BANTAM BOOKS
TORONTO · NEW YORK · LONDON · SYDNEY

LOVE'S DREAM
A Bantam Book/published by arrangement with
Robert Hale, Ltd.

PRINTING HISTORY
First published in Great Britain 1981
CIRCLE OF LOVE, the garland and the ring designs are
trademarks of Bantam Books, Inc.
Bantam edition/May 1982

ISBN 0-553-21514-0

Published simultaneously in the United States and Canada

PRINTED IN THE UNITED STATES OF AMERICA

0 9 8 7 6 5 4 3 2 1

One

The aircraft circled, awaiting instructions to land. Sharon Maine, from her window seat, caught glimpses of white buildings, wide streets and a vast expanse of water before the pilot made his final approach and they touched down with hardly a bump.

Sharon was feeling very excited at the propect of starting her new life in Australia, and as she stepped out onto the tarmac she could hardly believe she was really here in Adelaide.

She strained her eyes, trying to catch sight of her sister Julie, quite unaware of the admiring looks she was receiving from the male members of the airport staff.

She was a picture of health and beauty as she swung across to the airport buildings with her bag slung over her shoulder and carrying her overnight bag.

Her long shining silvery blonde hair lifted in the light breeze which tempered the hot sunshine bouncing off the tarmac. Her blue eyes sparkled with anticipation in her piquant face and a tiny smile played about her mouth.

It wasn't long before she cleared Customs, and went to collect the rest of her luggage.

"Shah, Shah!" a voice called, and Sharon looked up to see her sister Julie hurrying towards her, her face wreathed in smiles.

Sharon dropped her cases down and the two girls hugged and kissed each other delightedly.

"Shah, it is good to see you. How are you? Did you have a good flight? How was Daddy when you left?"

Sharon laughed. "Still the same old Julie. One thing at a time. You talk too much."

Julie grinned. "I can't help it. I am just made that way. Have you got your bags yet? You have? Good. Let's go then. We'll talk on the way. These yours?" she added, indicating the suitcases by Sharon's feet.

Sharon nodded, and Julie grabbed the two larger ones and strode off, leaving Sharon staring bemusedly after her, then suddenly realizing she would lose her sister if she didn't hurry up, picked up the remaining cases and ran after Julie.

Julie hasn't changed a bit, she thought affectionately. She had always been the lively one, whilst Sharon was more quiet and serious-minded. Now twenty-six, four years older than Sharon, she still looked like a teenager, and was as zany as ever.

Sharon finally caught up with Julie, just as she was leaving the terminal.

"Hang on a minute Ju," she panted. "Don't forget I don't know the way."

"What? Oh! Am I going too fast for you? I forgot you are an old slowcoach."

Sharon laughed. "Hey, not so much of the old, and I am not so slow either. It's you that is too quick."

"Never mind," Julie replied. "I will go your snail's pace instead. The car is parked over there."

With that she rushed off, completely forgetting her promise to slow down. Sharon had no alternative but to run after her, and by the time they had reached the car she was out of breath and perspiration stood out on her forehead.

"I am certainly glad we hadn't got any further to go," she said as she sank thankfully into the front passenger seat of the dark green Holden. "I am worn out, and feel so sticky."

"You aren't used to this heat," Julie replied with a grin. "You will soon adjust," she assured her.

"It isn't the heat I need to adjust to," Sharon muttered.

Julie only laughed. "You are out of practice, walking with me. It's been absolutely ages."

Yes, Sharon thought, three years. Three years since Julie had married Colin Martin, an Australian mining engineer she had met in London. They had only known each other for three months before Colin had had to return to Australia, so they had been married in order that Julie could return with him to his native land.

From Julie's glowing letters, Sharon knew the marriage was a good one, and couldn't help envying them their closeness.

Sharon had of course had boyfriends. With her looks she had attracted a lot of attention, but she had never found one man she would like to spend the rest of her life with.

Julie had always said that when she did fall in love it would be in a big way, with no half-measures.

Sharon shook herself out of her reverie at the sound of her sister's voice. "Pardon?" she said.

"You were miles away, Shah. Whatever were you thinking about?"

Sharon shrugged. "Oh, nothing much really. Just thinking of how happy you and Colin are, and wondering if I will be as lucky."

"No fear of that," Julie replied confidently. "You can have the pick of the men with your looks."

She grinned. "Not like me. I grabbed the first man who asked me in case I didn't get another chance."

"Come off it," Sharon scoffed. "You know as well as I do that you were never short of an escort, and you fell head over heels in love with Colin."

"Well, he thinks I am beautiful anyway," Julie said with satisfaction as a secret smile played about her lips.

"You are," Sharon agreed, looking her sister over. Julie was taller than Sharon's own five feet four inches, with a willowy slenderness and hair a couple of shades darker, which she had cut short and curled.

Julie always made out that she was jealous of Sharon's well-rounded figure, saying she must have wandered off the day they were handing out breasts, looking in disgust at her own slender shape.

"Don't be daft," Sharon had replied. "If you had a big bust you would be top heavy and would be falling flat on your face all the time."

The conversation had ended with both girls

rolling about, laughing at the picture Sharon had conjured up.

The car had been going steadily through the teeming streets of Adelaide as the girls talked, and soon they were pulling into a car park under a block of flats.

"Well here we are Shah, home," Julie said. Together they unloaded Sharon's cases and went up in the lift to the third floor.

Julie unlocked the door and motioned Sharon in, calling, "Colin, are you about?"

There was no reply. "He isn't back yet," she stated unnecessarily. "Come on, let's stow your cases in your room, then we'll have a nice cup of tea."

Sharon followed her sister down the hall and into a fair-sized bedroom.

"Oh, it is lovely," she exclaimed involuntarily. The bedroom was furnished with a natural pine dressing-table and chest of drawers. Flowered curtains matched the bedspreads on the twin beds, with a thick piled burnt-orange carpet covering the floor.

"Thank you," Julie replied, smiling at the compliment. "We had a lovely time furnishing the whole apartment really."

She walked over to the double doors painted in a fawn shade. "The wardrobes are built in, so it allows more free space," she explained. "Anyway, you can unpack later. Let's go and have that cup of tea."

Sharon looked down ruefully at her once crisp blue linen trouser suit which she had put on at the last stop-over.

"I could do with changing out of these clothes," she said. "They seem to have got rather limp, like me, and I need a wash."

"No problem, Shah. The bathroom is just across

5

the hall. You get yourself sorted out and I'll give you a shout when the tea is ready."

Left alone, Sharon began unlocking her suitcases, lying out a pair of pale blue denim jeans and white short-sleeved teeshirt, then collecting her toilet things, crossed the hall into the bathroom.

Decorated in blue and white, the bathroom was cool and attractive. The pale blue bathroom suite was shown off to perfection against the dark blue and white tiles. In the corner Sharon noticed a shower unit and looked at it longingly.

Stepping out into the hall again, she called, "Ju, have I got time for a shower?"

"Help yourself," her sister's voice came from the far end of the hall. "There is no hurry. The tea will wait."

As Sharon stood under the shower a few minutes later, she marvelled at her change of circumstances. If Daddy hadn't suddenly decided to re-marry, she thought, I would probably still be living at home to run the house, as well as holding my job down in the local library.

Julie and Sharon's mother had died six years earlier, and after Julie had married there was only Sharon and her father left. They were very close, but Sharon had been pleased when her father had told her diffidently that he had met another woman, and asked if she minded if he brought her round to dinner one evening.

Louise had turned out to be a charming widow, just a few years younger than Mr. Maine, and she and Sharon had hit it off right from the beginning.

As the weeks went by, Sharon had seen how close Louise and her father had become, and it came as no real surprise when Mr. Maine had said he had asked Louise to marry him.

Sharon had been delighted, agreeing it was time he enjoyed life again, then promptly sat down to write to Julie to tell her the news.

Julie had written straight back with congratulations to her father, and an invitation for Sharon to join her and Colin in Australia, either for an extended holiday or to live permanently.

Sharon, privately agreeing with Julie that their father and his new wife would probably want to be on their own, told her father that she had decided it was about time she saw a bit more of the world, and what better place to start than in Australia. After arguing half-heartedly, her father had finally agreed, but Sharon knew he was pleased really.

Only three months had passed since then, and after the wedding Sharon had made all the necessary arrangements, and at last she was here in Australia. She hadn't made up her mind as to how long she would stay. It depended on how a number of things worked out.

As Sharon was dressing she heard her brother-in-law's voice calling, "Ju, where are you? I have some great news."

Sharon emerged from her room a few minutes later, feeling really refreshed. She made her way down the hall, finding Julie and Colin in the kitchen, talking animatedly.

"Hello Colin. How's things?" she asked.

Colin broke off from what he was saying to Julie to stride over and envelope Sharon in a bear hug, his face wreathed in smiles. He then stood back, holding her hands and looking her up and down.

"It's great to see you," he said. "You are more beautiful than I remembered. If I wasn't already shackled to that beaut over there I'd have you instead."

Sharon laughed, enjoying the banter. "You aren't my type," she retorted. "I prefer dark-haired men."

Colin ran a hand through his own thick fair hair. "That's that then," he said ruefully. "You wouldn't mind just a flirtation with me though, would you?" he added, grabbing her again.

"Unhand my sister," Julie demanded imperiously.

"Oh dear, I wish I was single," Colin said mockingly, shaking his head. "You stop all my fun."

"Not quite all," Julie said slyly, her eyes full of mischief.

"Later, sweet," Colin promised with a grin. "Now then, where is my tea? I could die of thirst for all you care."

Julie threw a towel at him, telling him that if he was that desperate, he could get it himself, and while he was at it he could pour one for her and Sharon.

"Come on Sharon, let's go and make ourselves comfortable in the sitting-room. It will be nice to be waited on for a change."

She threw an arched look at Colin before flouncing out of the kitchen. Colin looked sadly at Sharon, raising his hands in the air. "Don't you feel sorry for me, Sharon?" he asked. "Your sister leads me a terrible life."

Sharon laughed. "No I most certainly do not," she replied as she followed Julie. "You know very well she spoils you."

"Tea is served, your ladyships," Colin said when he joined the girls a couple of minutes later. He put the tray on the low table then flopped back in the chair. "I will need to put my feet up for half an hour now. That has worn me out."

"Shut up and drink your tea," Julie told him.

"Yes, boss," Colin agreed meekly.

"You have come at just the right time Shah," Julie remarked. If you had arrived a couple of weeks later we wouldn't have been here."

Sharon turned surprised eyes to her sister. "Whatever do you mean?" she asked.

"You explain, Colin," Julie said. "I can get it straight myself then."

"Sure thing, sweet. We are moving up north for a year, to just outside Darwin," he explained.

"You never mentioned it in your letters, Ju," Sharon interrupted.

Julie laughed. "I didn't know myself until a few minutes ago. I am as surprised as you are. It will be great fun though, won't it. I wonder where we will live. I hope we get on with the neighbours."

"Why are you going Colin?" Sharon interrupted her sister's flow of chatter.

"If my dearest wife would allow it, I will tell you," he answered with a resigned look on his face as he looked at Julie.

"The floor is yours," Julie replied. "I will be as quiet as a mouse."

Colin issued what sounded remarkably like a snort. "Some hope of that," he muttered, then had to endure being punched playfully by Julie, much to Sharon's amusement. They are a super couple, she thought, then concentrated on what Colin was saying.

"As you know, I am lecturing on mining techniques at the university at the moment."

Sharon nodded. Colin was an expert in his field, even though he was only thirty.

"Well," he continued, "I have got the chance to go to work at one of the mining research centres up in the Northern Territories. It is a great chance for me. I knew there was a post becoming vacant up there. I put in for it but didn't really expect anything to come of it. You can imagine how surprised I was when one of the directors came to see me to offer me the post. Apparently the guy who was retiring soon was taken ill suddenly, so he packed it in now instead. So," he finished up, "we are expected in two weeks time."

"Congratulations, Colin. You deserve the opportunity," Sharon said sincerely. "But," she added, disappointment clouding her voice, "you won't want to drag me along with you. It will be allright if I stay at this flat and get myself a job, won't it?"

"No," Colin and Julie chorused. "You don't think we would leave you here on your own, do you?" Colin added. "You must have a low opinion of us."

"Oh no, I didn't mean it like that," Sharon replied quickly. "What I meant was that quarters will be provided for you, won't they? They won't expect me as well."

"Then we'll live somewhere else," Julie said loyally. "I am certainly not losing you as soon as you have got here."

Colin put his large hand over Sharon's, resting on the table. "We want you with us, O.K.? No more arguments."

Sharon nodded, feeling ridiculously near to tears as she heard the sincerity in his voice.

"That's settled then," Julie said with a sigh. "Well, I can't sit here talking all day. I have got a lot of organizing to do, not least of all feeding us before we starve, or we won't be going anywhere."

The following two weeks flew by in a whirlwind of activity. Sharon's offer to take over the running of the apartment, leaving Julie free for other things, was welcomed after a bit of persuasion.

Colin had been lucky enough to find a tenant for the apartment, a young member of the university staff who wanted to get married. Colin knew the man well, and felt assured that the apartment would be kept looking as nice as when they left it.

Finally, all was sorted out and the time arrived for them to leave. They boarded the plane in high spirits, and four and a half hours later they touched down at Darwin.

They alighted from the plane to a wet tarmac. They discovered there had been a tropical downpour before they arrived, but already the ground was drying rapidly in the hot sun, sending up clouds of steam into the air.

A representative of the Research Centre which Colin was joining met them in the airport lounge. Middle-aged, with greying hair, he introduced himself as Jim Davies.

Colin introduced Julie and Sharon, and Jim beamed jovially at them.

"You lucky guy," he said to Colin with a twinkle in his eye. "Fancy having two such beauts to see to your comfort."

"To pester me to death, more like." Colin laughed, then added ruefully, "Yes, they're allright to look at, but boy, can they talk."

"How dare you," Julie said indignantly, but couldn't keep a straight face, spoiling it by laughing out loud.

"Are you ready?" Jim asked, still chuckling. "The company has booked you into the Queen's Hotel for a few days. I hope you don't mind, but it will only be for a few days I assure you, just until your bungalow is ready for occupation."

"A place to eat and lay our heads is all we need," Julie answered. "We're not hard to please."

They followed Jim out to his car, a grey convertible with the hood down. Jim pointed to this. "Do you want the top up?"

"No thanks," Colin replied for all of them. "The fresh air will do us good."

"Isn't it fantastic?" Sharon said as they bowled along the wide bright streets. Her eyes sparkled with pleasure. "I've never seen anything like it, have you, Ju?"

For once, Julie seemed lost for words, much to Colin's amusement. He had to agree though that Darwin was a marvellous city.

The entire place seemed alive with colour. Everywhere they looked there were flowers in every shade of the rainbow and the bright green foliage surrounding them set them off to perfection. The gardens of the attractive modern buildings were a riot of fragipani and poinsettias, and they were thrilled to see palm trees growing everywhere.

"It's beautiful," Julie eventually breathed. "And what about that heavenly scent?"

The air was heady with the mixed scents of the different flowers, and combined with the tang of the sea formed a unique smell, never to be forgotten. Jim told them that stories have it that sailors from Darwin could detect the smell of their home port whilst still miles out to sea.

"You are seeing it at the best time," he said. "We

get plenty of storms this time of the year. They are heavy, but don't last long, and they do wonders for the vegetation. New growth will spring up in next to no time."

"It really is gorgeous," Julie said. "I am sure we are going to like living here."

"You sure will, Mrs. Martin," Jim answered.

"Please call me Julie," she told him. "I feel so old when I am called Misses," she added, grinning up at her husband.

"You should have stayed single then, love," Colin replied, "then you wouldn't have that problem."

"You might feel it Julie," Jim replied gallantly, "but you sure don't look it. You hardly look old enough to be married at all."

Julie's eyes twinkled, and she laughed happily. "Flattery will get you everywhere. I am absolutely certain I am going to like it here if all the men are as charming as you," she told him, bringing a slight flush to his cheeks.

"We're noted for it," he replied nonchalantly, the colour under his tan belieing his casual tone.

They arrived safely at the Queen's Hotel, and Jim accompanied them to the lobby. After procuring their keys he asked them if they would join him for dinner that evening, to which request they readily agreed.

Sharon's room was opposite to the one allotted to Julie and Colin. It was pleasant, with bright patterned curtains and bedspread, and fluffy rugs on the polished wooden floors. The furniture was light pine, which made the room look bigger than it actually was. The adjoining bathroom was small and compact, but Sharon was pleased to see there was a shower unit.

After showering she slipped on a silk kimono, beautifully patterned in blues and greens, then wandered over to the window. She gazed out over the white buildings and colourful gardens to where the sun glinted on the sparkling blue sea.

Feeling suddenly that she was being watched, Sharon dropped her gaze to the hotel gardens, meeting the amused expression of the tanned face of a tall dark-haired man standing smoking a cigar just in front of her window. She suddenly realized she was staring as the stranger lifted his eyebrows sardonically.

Sharon felt herself blushing and hurriedly stepped back out of sight.

Of all the cheek, she thought, standing there staring at me. Perhaps that's how he gets his kicks. She shrugged her shoulders, and resisting the sudden impulse to have another look to see if he was still there, began to dress for dinner.

She chose a long flowing dress in midnight blue silk, but even the wide cut of the dress could not hide her curves. She applied a light make-up, then twisted her hair into a chic chignon. Looking in the full length mirror before she left, she was more than pleased with the final result.

Just at that moment a knock came on the door and she heard Julie's calling, "Are you ready, Shah?"

"Just coming," Sharon replied, and grabbing her purse, hurried out.

They arrived in the lobby to find Jim Davies already waiting for them, and he came forward to greet them with a beaming smile.

"Ah, there you are," he said unnecessarily. "What about a drink?"

When they nodded assent he suggested the girls

go through to the lounge to find a table whilst he and Colin fetched the drinks from the bar.

The menfolk weren't long, and soon all four of them were settled and chatting happily. Jim spent some time telling Colin about the Research Centre, getting really enthusiastic about the uranium that was being mined in Rum Jungle, not far away.

Julie knew from experience that once the men started talking shop, there wasn't much that would stop them.

"It was always the same when we were out with people from the university," she explained to Sharon. "They take us out for a good time, and we end up sitting like a load of wallflowers until one of the men remembers we're with them."

Sharon laughed. "It isn't that bad, surely?"

"Do you know, it gets so bad that I sometimes think if we were pieces of metal we would be better off."

"Did you say something, Ju?" Colin asked.

The girls laughed at each other. Julie laid a hand on Colin's arm, saying, "No dear, just admiring the decor."

"That's all right then," Colin replied, turning back to Jim to ask about the computers used in some mine."

Julie lifted her eyes expressively. "See what I mean?"

Sharon nodded. "Perhaps you would be better off if you were a piece of metal," she told her.

Julie grinned cheekily. "At least he would get hold of me now and again."

A few minutes later they went into dinner, and the talk at last became general, with Jim telling them the best places of interest in the area.

"What do you say to a dance, Julie," Jim asked, after they had finished their meal.

"Try to stop me," Julie replied with a grin.

"I am not much of a hand at dancing," Colin said ruefully, "but if you want to risk bruised feet, we'll give it a go."

"I'll risk it," Sharon smiled, but inwardly hoping it wouldn't be that bad.

As it turned out, she needn't have had any qualms on that score. Colin, like many big men, was light on his feet, and Sharon enjoyed the dance.

Jim and Julie returned to the table at the same time as Sharon and Colin, and they mutually decided to sit the next one out and have another drink.

"How's it going, Jim?" a voice said.

Sharon looked up to see a tall man standing next to the table, his hand on Jim's shoulder. This stranger was certainly an outdoor man, she thought seeing the dark-tanned face and large capable hands, and she couldn't help admiring his good looks and slim athletic body.

"Pete," Jim cried joyously. "What are you doing here? Let you off the leash, has he?"

Pete grinned down at him. "No, he's here with me. We came up for a conference and to go to the Agency to fix up some secretarial help for the station."

"Well, it's great seeing you," Jim told him. "Let me introduce you to these folks. Colin Martin, who is joining the staff at the Centre, his wife Julie, and Julie's sister Sharon, just over from England. Folks, this is Pete Weston, playboy, womanizer and drunkard when he is away from home, but sober and hardworking when he is at home."

Seeing the dumbfounded looks on the faces of his guests, he roared with laughter.

"That sure was some introduction, Jim," Pete said with a grin. "I'll do the same thing for you one day."

"Come and join us Pete," Jim invited. "What'll you have, a beer?"

"Sure, thanks," Pete replied, pulling up another chair.

"Actually, Pete isn't quite what I made him out to be," Jim felt obliged to explain. "I had better put the record straight here and now, before you get the wrong idea. Pete's family owns one of the biggest cattle stations in the Northern Territories, Weston Downs, down by the Alice."

"The Alice?" Sharon queried.

"Alice Springs," Pete explained. "The heart of Australia, dead centre of the continent. Greatest place in the world," he added proudly.

"There speaks a descendant of one of the pioneer families of the Outback," Jim said. "How's your Mother, Pete?"

Pete's face dropped slightly. "She hasn't been too well recently," he replied soberly. "She says it's her age, but we think it is something more. Trouble is, she won't see the doc."

"You mean Nat hasn't made her see him?" Jim asked in surprise.

"Mother is the only person he doesn't get his own way with," Pete told him. "He is totally different with her, very gentle."

Jim said, "Nat is Pete's older brother, and he runs the station. He is a hard man, but never asks a man to do anything he wouldn't do himself. The stockmen who work the Outback stations are a hard lot of men, and it needs a strong-willed boss to keep them in line. Nat commands respect from the hardest of them."

"Proper tyrant by the sound of it," Sharon quipped. "Does he treat his wife the same?"

"He isn't married," Pete answered. He grinned. "Actually, I am waiting for the day when some woman brings him to his knees. The only woman he appreciates is Mother though. Many a sheila has tried to snare him, one way or another. He takes everything that is offered. What man in his position wouldn't? He gives nothing of himself though."

"That brother of yours sounds selfish and conceited," Sharon said without thinking.

"Someone taking my name in vain?" a hard deep voice asked from directly behind Sharon's chair.

Sharon looked up and caught her breath in dismay, the colour running up into her face, for the man standing there was none other than her 'peeping Tom' of earlier in the evening.

Two

"Oh no," she breathed.

"Nat, good to see you," Jim said, taking Nat's attention from Sharon, much to her relief.

The two men shook hands, and Jim began again with the round of introductions. When Nat took Sharon's hand, he squeezed it harder than was necessary, and Sharon's embarrassment turned to anger, as she looked up at him with defiance in her blue eyes.

"How do you do, Mr. Weston?" she asked sweetly, but making it absolutely clear that she couldn't care less.

"From what I have just heard," he said quietly, "better than you'd like me to be."

Sharon opened her eyes wide. "I can't think what you mean by that," she said innocently.

"Hey, what are you two whispering about?" Pete asked suspiciously.

"Just asking Miss-er-Sharon to dance," Nat replied suavely. "Come on, Sharon, our music awaits us."

"I don't think . . . ," Sharon began, but Nat squeezed her shoulder until she winced. She decided there was nothing to be gained by making a scene in front of the others, so got reluctantly to her feet to allow him to lead her towards the dance floor. As they left, she heard Pete say, "How about that? What's got into Nat?"

Sharon's temper was now reaching boiling point. She had never been treated like that before. How dared he? she thought.

Nat swung her into his arms as the band struck up a waltz. Sharon held herself stiffly, trying desperately to keep her distance and her temper.

"Relax, honey," Nat whispered into her ear.

"You are insufferable," Sharon replied through clenched teeth.

"Is that what you think?" he asked mockingly. "We'll have to try and change your opinion then."

Suddenly his grip tightened and he pulled her close up against his hard body. Sharon tried to pull away, but to no avail. Nat's arms were like two steel bands.

"Let me go," Sharon hissed, her eyes flashing, but Nat only laughed softly.

"When I'm ready, and not before," he told her.

As they danced past the open french windows, Nat suddenly changed direction, guiding her out through them onto the darkened terrace.

"What do you think you are doing?" Sharon demanded.

"Just trying to change your opinion of me," he replied suavely. "You really shouldn't form an opinion until you know all aspects."

Before Sharon knew what was happening, Nat's one hand was tangled in her hair, whilst he forced her head back with the other.

Her cry was cut off almost before it started as his mouth descended on hers in a hard and punishing kiss.

Sharon tried to escape the embrace, but she was no match for Nat's strength. Deciding she might just as well save her energy, she went limp in his arms. Her action caused Nat to change his tactics, and his kiss became tender, teasing her mouth until her lips parted in response. The kiss deepened, and Sharon found herself floating on a cloud of feeling.

Her body became fluid and she was moulded against his male hardness, and her arms crept up round his neck of their own volition. Everything was blocked out except the exquisite tingles of ecstasy which attacked her whole body.

It came as a great shock when Nat put her firmly away from him, chuckling contentedly. "That's better," he said softly. "I knew I could change your opinion of me if I tried hard enough."

Sharon had never felt so humiliated in her life before. She wished the ground would open up and swallow her. Her pleasure in the embrace turned to burning anger. She looked up at him, her eyes sparkling with tears of anger and shame.

"You swine," she said. "You are nothing but a selfish and conceited swine."

To her chagrin, all he did was smile. "Well, that is what you told my brother I was, and that was before

21

you had met me. I have just confirmed it, so you should be happy you were right. You'll have to forget about the part in between though. You thought quite differently for a while. Shall we go in?"

Sharon turned and marched back into the room, her head held high. By the time they reached the table where the others were she had herself under control, the only sign of her agitation the two spots of bright red on her cheeks and her glittering eyes.

Julie looked curiously at her sister, but for once said nothing. She would get to the bottom of it later, she thought. It was left to Pete to ask what had happened to them.

"We lost sight of the pair of you and thought we had been deserted," he added with a knowing grin.

Sharon didn't know what to say, but could feel the colour running up into her face. She felt embarrassed, knowing what Pete was thinking, but Nat wasn't a bit bothered. "Sharon felt a bit faint, so we stepped outside for a breath of air. Didn't we, Sharon?" he added, his hand squeezing her arm in warning.

"Yes-yes of course," she confirmed, holding her head down.

"Are you feeling better now?" Colin asked in concern.

Sharon felt bad about deceiving everyone, but nevertheless managed to smile across at Colin. "Yes, I'm fine now," she replied. "It was just that it was so warm in here."

"You will soon get used to the heat," Jim said jovially. "It must get you down after the cold in England."

Sharon murmured something in agreement, then the talk became general. Sharon was very quiet and didn't dare look at Nat for fear of the mockery she would see in his face. She was too full of her own thoughts to notice the strange looks she was receiving from her sister.

The evening broke up a little later, with Jim promising to call for Colin to take him to the Research Centre to look around the following day.

When Sharon shook hands with Pete, he leaned towards her. "Can I take you sightseeing tomorrow, Sharon," he asked.

Sharon was about to demur when she happened to catch sight of the mocking expression on Nat's face, so instead she gave Pete a brilliant smile. "I would love that Pete, thank you. See you about ten in the morning if that is all right with you."

"Sure thing, Sharon," he answered, his face lighting up.

Sharon stole a glance at Nat's face, and was pleased to see he was now frowning, which was replaced by a bland expression when he saw her looking at him. "Goodnight, Sharon," was all he said though. "I'll be seeing you."

"Goodnight," she replied stiffly, adding under her breath, not if I see you first.

As Sharon was getting ready for bed she was surprised to hear a knock on the door. She was startled, and called sharply, "Who is it?"

"Only me, Shah," Julie's voice came through the door. "Can I come in for a minute?"

Sharon opened the door to admit her sister. "What is it, Ju?" she asked.

"That is what I would like to know," Julie answered. "What went on between you and Nat Weston when you disappeared?"

The colour ran up Sharon's face but she replied nonchalantly, "Nothing. I don't know what you mean."

"Come off it, Shah. When you came back you looked just about ready to commit murder."

Sharon knew that Julie wouldn't give up easily. "All right, so he made me mad. He is a conceited swine."

Julie looked shocked, then laughed. "My, what language. He must really have got your back up. What did he say to you—or do?" she added suspiciously.

"We just had a few words," Sharon replied wearily, resisting the sudden temptation to tell her sister to mind her own business. "Now, if you don't mind, I am tired out. We'll talk in the morning, all right?"

She threw a smile at Julie, who after a slight hesitation, shrugged her shoulders. "O.K. If that's the way you want it. Goodnight, Shah. Sleep well."

"Goodnight, Ju," Sharon replied. She heaved a sigh of relief when she was on her own again. Ju wasn't really a nosey person, she decided. It was just that she was concerned for her.

Her thoughts turned once more to Nat Weston. What a nerve he had. The truth was that she had never met anyone so overbearing before. Close on the heels of that came the memory of his kiss, and she was ashamed of her own response to it. How could anyone dislike a man, yet still fall under the spell of his love-making?

She had been kissed a good many times before, but never had any man's love-making had such an overwhelming effect on her senses. In fact she had never liked excessive petting, and couldn't understand what had come over her.

She put a hand to her lips, reliving the experience

of Nat's kiss. She found herself wondering what it would be like to be loved by a man like him. The experience would be shattering, she guessed. He had tremendous sex-appeal, and just look how a kiss had affected her. If he went further than a kiss . . .

Here she pulled herself up short. Whatever is the matter with me, she thought. I hate him. I don't want to get involved in an affair with him.

With great difficulty she managed to adjust her thoughts, and snuggled down into the soft bed. It was a long time though before sleep overtook her.

Sharon awoke next morning feeling really refreshed. Her thoughts turned immediately to Nat, but she resolutely shook them off and concentrated on wondering where Pete would be taking her today.

No sign of the turmoil of the night showed on her face when she joined Julie and Colin at the breakfast table. She was gay and laughing, joining in the banter between them. Julie looked at her oddly once or twice, but didn't bring up the subject of the night before at all.

"I wonder what time Jim will be here?" she asked.

"He said he would be here pretty early," Colin replied with a smile. "He can't wait to get us there. He is really keen to show us round the place."

Julie laughed. "And you are just as keen to see it," she told him. "I expect you will forget all about me when we get there."

"Only during the day, honey," was Colin's quick rejoinder, leering at her.

Julie rolled her eyes. "Promises, promises," she laughed.

"See what I have to put up with, Sharon?" Colin mourned. "I am married to a brazen madam."

"You wouldn't have her any other way," Sharon replied with a smile, "so don't try to tell me otherwise."

"Too right," Colin agreed. "Ah, here's Jim now," he added.

"Morning, girls," Jim said breezily. "I didn't dream you then. You are a pair of beauts."

Everyone laughed at his nonsense. "Ready, Colin?" he added. "The sooner we start, the sooner we get there."

"Sure thing, sport," Colin replied. "Are you ready, girls?"

Julie got to her feet at once. "I can't wait to get to our future home."

She glanced at Sharon, still sitting there, a stricken look on her face.

"What's the matter, Shah?" she asked, suddenly looking concerned.

"I am ever so sorry, Ju," Sharon replied. "I didn't realize you wanted me to come too. I have arranged to go out sightseeing."

Julie raised her eyebrows. "Going out? Who are you going with, Nat Weston?"

Sharon shook her head. "Oh no, of course not. Pete asked me to go out with him."

"Oh I see," Julie said. "Never mind, you can come another time. We won't be able to do anything at the bungalow anyway. I am only going along to meet the other folks."

Sharon smiled at her sister. "I'll put him off if you want me to come with you. I'm not all that bothered about going."

Julie waved her hands airily. "No way, Shah. You go and enjoy yourself. We'll see you this evening."

"Don't do anything I wouldn't do," Colin warned Sharon, his eyes alight with mischief.

Sharon raised her eyebrows expressively. "That leaves me a considerable choice then," she answered cheekily, and they parted, still laughing.

Sharon didn't have long to wait before Pete arrived. She could see how he got his reputation with women. He really was a good-looker. His tall athletic body was shown off to perfection in a pair of fawn slacks and brown sweat shirt.

"Hello, Pete," Sharon said shyly.

"Hi there, honey," he replied. "My, you look good enough to eat. Pity I've already had breakfast."

Sharon blushed at the admiration in his eyes, but couldn't help but be pleased by the compliment. She knew she looked pretty good. Her tight-fitting white slacks and yellow skinny rib shirt showed off her figure well, and with her hair tied back in a pony tail and only a touch of make-up she looked fresh and neat.

"Where are we going, Pete?" she asked eagerly as they went out into the brilliant sunshine.

"Well, seeing as you are a newcomer I thought we would stay pretty local. There are some great spots around here," he replied.

"Are you sure you won't be bored," Sharon asked uncertainly. "You must have seen them hundreds of times."

Pete slipped his arm casually around her shoulders. "Not with you though, honey."

"Flatterer," she replied with a smile, making him smile.

Pete proved to be a marvellous companion, and Sharon was pleased she hadn't turned him down as she had intended. He was gay and teasing, and Sharon spent most of the day laughing. He certainly knows how to keep a woman entertained, she thought. His manner was open and casual, asking nothing more than good company and friendship for the most part.

They went first right onto the cliffs from where a panoramic view of the area was possible. Sharon caught her breath in wonderment as she looked down the steep cliff face to the natural harbour where vessels of every shape and size could be seen. The small boats bobbed gently at their moorings, just as attractive as the bigger and more stylish craft.

The brilliant blue of the sky merged with the deeper shades of the ocean, whilst the sun's rays were reflected and re-reflected in the rippling water.

"Isn't it beautiful, Pete?" Sharon sighed, her face alight with pleasure and her eyes sparkling.

"Too right, girl," he replied. "The sea is a wondrous thing, even during a storm. All that uncontrolled energy, with the waves rising high in the air and the water changing colour. It sure is a magnificent sight."

"I hope to see that before we return," Sharon said.

"We're coming to the end of the 'wet' season now, but you'll still be around come the end of the year, won't you? We get the worst weather between October and December."

"We're here for a year," Sharon answered. "That is, Colin and Julie are. I don't know about me. I haven't decided what to do yet. I might move on and take a look at New Zealand."

"You haven't seen anything of Australia yet. You

should spend some time in my part of the country. There is nothing in the world to beat it," Pete added proudly. "The Outback is a world of its own. It's hard country, but all the hard work involved in surviving there is worthwhile."

"You never know, Pete, I might turn up on your doorstep one of these days. Perhaps I can get a job there."

"What do you do?" Pete asked.

"I'm a librarian really, but I can also do shorthand and typing and filing, that sort of thing. I could always get a job in an office if there were no library vacancies."

Sharon was too busy watching the ocean to see the speculative look come into Pete's face. However, all he said was, "I'm sure anybody would be pleased to have you around, whether you could type or not."

Sharon laughed. "You'll have me quite vain if you carry on like that."

"Just the truth, honey," Pete told her seriously. "Now, how about a swim?"

"I'll have to go back to the hotel for my costume. Will we still have time?"

"Sure thing, but I know a nice secluded place where you wouldn't need a costume," Pete answered with a grin.

Sharon punched him playfully, although she couldn't control the slight flush in her cheeks.

"We'll have less of that," she laughed. "I'm a good girl."

"Good at what, though, that's what I'd like to know," Pete replied instantly.

Sharon raised her hands. "What is it with you Australian guys? You sound just like Colin."

"What?" Pete cried. "Your brother-in-law wants to find out what you are good at, too? I think I had better have a word with your sister."

"Oh shut up," Sharon said. "Let's go back and get my costume."

"Oh dear," Pete answered in mock disappointment. "Foiled again. I'm not going to get my wicked way with you after all."

"Well not yet," Sharon replied without thinking, then put her hand to her mouth as she realized what she had implied.

"Well now," Peter drawled. "I'll stick around for a while. Perhaps my luck will change."

Sharon looked startled for a moment, then seeing the teasing light in his eyes, laughed, revelling in his uncomplicated humour. They wandered back to the hotel hand in hand, happy in each other's company.

"It's fantastic," Sharon marvelled. "The colours of the flowers here have to be seen to be believed, and as for the scents . . ."

She feasted her eyes on the masses of tropical foliage in the gardens as they strolled along. The brilliantly coloured flowers such as the poinsettias and frangipani, surrounded by all the greenery, showed up to perfection against the brilliant white of the modern attractive buildings.

Everywhere there was a sense of space and light. The streets were wide with palm trees waving their fronds in the light breeze. To Sharon, used to narrow crowded streets and dark dismal weather, it was like being in Paradise. She tried to explain her feelings to Pete.

"You think it is spacious here?" Pete asked. "Wait until you come to the interior. That is what I call spacious. It's like being alone in the world. I get claustrophobic if I am in the city too long. It is great to visit the bright lights, but better still to get back home."

Sharon couldn't imagine what it was about the Outback which instilled such fervour in Pete. He seemed so much at home in the city. She sighed unconsciously.

Pete glanced at her quickly. "Something wrong, honey?" he asked.

Sharon shook off the sudden feeling of melancholy which had overtaken her for no apparent reason, and smiled brightly.

"Not a thing," she replied gaily. "I'm not used to all this," she added, waving her free hand all around her.

"You soon will be," Pete promised. "Ah, here we are. Don't be long getting your gear. I am an impatient man."

"Yes, sir," Sharon replied, dashing into the hotel and running into what felt like a brick wall.

"Oh, sorry," she said automatically, as two strong arms came out to support her. She looked up to meet the mocking gaze of Nat Weston.

"You," she breathed.

"You just can't resist throwing yourself at me, can you?" he taunted.

Sharon's face flamed and her eyes glittered angrily. "That will be the day," she retorted. "Now will you let go of me?"

"Hey Nat, what are you doing with my girl?" Peter asked with a grin, as he strolled up to them.

Nat raised his eyebrows at the possessive note underlying the humour in Pete's voice.

"I bumped into him," Sharon explained quickly.

"And a very pleasant experience it was too," Nat added, a wicked glint in his eye.

Sharon stepped away from him, her head held high. "I won't be long, Pete. Don't go away."

"Not until I have had my wicked way with you," Pete leered.

Sharon could quite cheerfully have strangled him for saying that in front of Nat. As she walked away she heard Nat ask angrily. "Now what the hell did you mean by that?"

She didn't hear Pete's reply, but hoped for some unknown reason that he explained to Nat that it was only a joke. Why she didn't want Nat to get the wrong impression she couldn't explain.

Three

"Where are we going?" Sharon asked as they drove along in the sleek open sports car.

"There are quite a few great beaches within easy reach, but I thought we'd go out to Casuarina," Pete replied.

"As in trees?" Sharon asked with a smile.

"You got it first time," Pete told her. "That is how it got its name. I thought we would have a swim, get something to eat, then laze the rest of the day away."

"Sounds marvellous," Sharon agreed happily.

Soon Pete was parking the car and Sharon got her first glimpse of the beach. It was just as she had imagined a tropical island to be. A great expanse of silver sand, shaded in places by huge palm trees, ran down to the blue of the sea. Waves rolled gently onto the beach, their movement in the bright sunshine having an unmistakable beauty.

Sharon turned to Pete and dropped him a light kiss on his cheek. "Oh Pete, thank you for bringing me here. It's beautiful."

"So was that little gesture of affection, ma'am. Allow me to return the compliment."

Pete pulled her into his arms and kissed her gently on the mouth. Sharon returned the slight pressure before she pulled away. Somewhere in the back of her mind was the memory of a quite different kiss, but she resolutely pushed the thought away.

"Come on," she cried gaily. "Don't let's waste a minute."

She grabbed her towel and ran down to the beach. Dropping her towel and beach robe she ran down to dive into the ocean's warm translucent water. Pete was soon beside her and they spent a happy hour in the water, splashing around like a couple of school-children, then spread out their towels and lay down on them to dry off.

They lay in silence, each happy with their own thoughts, until Pete leaned over Sharon to kiss her gently. Sharon's eyes flew open to see his face close to hers.

"You'd better not lay out too long at one go," he said seriously. "I'd hate that beautiful body of yours to get sunburnt."

Sharon blushed as Pete's eyes travelled down her body, taking in the curves barely covered by her blue bikini and the well-shaped legs. His admiring glance deepened into something else and he lowered his head to kiss her again. Sharon returned the kiss, enjoying the attention, but expecting him to keep it light.

To her dismay his kiss became more demanding

and his hand slid up her body, finishing up on her breast.

"No!" she cried, rolling away.

Pete looked at her in amazement. "What's the matter? Did I hurt you?" he asked anxiously.

"N-no," Sharon replied, pulling herself together. "Sorry, Pete," she added. "I don't know what came over me."

"Was it because I touched you," he persisted. "I'm sorry if I upset you. Most girls take it as a matter of course, and you seemed to enjoy kissing me."

Sharon took pity on his confusion, laying a hand gently on his arm. "Don't get me wrong, Pete, please. I did enjoy kissing you, but I am not most girls, as you put it. Oh, how can I explain? I like you a lot, but that's as far as it goes. That's as far as it's gone with all my boyfriends."

Suddenly she put her head in her hands. "I don't know what's wrong with me," she cried. "I think I must be frigid or something. I just don't like all the petting and sex that is the in thing nowadays."

Pete put his arms around her and held her gently against him. "I've got the feeling you are a one-man girl, honey. When you fall in love you won't feel like this. You will want the lucky guy to touch you, and probably crave for more."

"I hope you're right, Pete," she sighed. She was quiet for a few moments then looked up at him, her eyes bright with unshed tears. "You're a nice guy, Pete, and I just wish it was you I'd fallen in love with." She smiled mistily at him and then pressed her lips fleetingly to his. "Right then, what's next?" she asked brightly.

Following her lead, Pete changed the subject. "I for one am hungry. Let's get something to eat, then have a doze in the shade of those palms over there. Then we'll swim again before we make tracks for the hotel. How does that sound?"

"Great," she replied, jumping up and brushing the sand off herself. She missed the sad look on Pete's face as he looked at her.

The rest of the day followed the schedule Pete had planned, and they got back to the hotel in time to change for dinner.

Before they parted, Pete took Sharon's hands and looked down at her tenderly. "No hard feelings, honey?"

"None," she replied promptly.

"Will you come out with me again tomorrow?" Pete asked. "I promise to behave myself."

"I believe you," Sharon replied with a smile, "and I'd love to come."

"How about going down to the Woolwonga Aboriginal Reserve, and stopping overnight? No strings attached, I promise," he added quickly, when he caught her wary look.

Sharon hesitated, wondering what Julie would say to it, then decided it had got nothing to do with her.

"All right Pete, you're on. It sounds exciting."

"Right then. I'll pick you up at nine-thirty, so be ready." Pete warned her with a grin.

"You can tell me more during dinner this evening," Sharon said.

Pete's face dropped. "I'm sorry, honey, I shan't be here for dinner this evening. Nat and I are going over to a friend's place."

"Never mind. We've got our trip to look forward to. See you in the morning," Sharon told him.

"Too right," Pete grinned, and left Sharon to make her way to her room. She had only just slipped her shoes off when Julie came to see her.

"How was your day, Shah?" she asked.

Sharon smiled. "Marvellous thanks. Pete is good company. How did you get on at the Centre?"

"The people are super. Everybody was so friendly and welcoming. I shall enjoy being there," Julie replied.

"Did you have a good look at the bungalow?" Sharon asked.

Julie's face clouded over and she looked rather uncomfortable. "It's very nice. All modern conveniences."

"But . . ?" Sharon prompted. "I can tell something is wrong."

"I don't quite know how to say it," Julie replied.

"Straight out, that's best," Sharon said promptly.

"It is a bit difficult." Julie hesitated, then burst out, "It has only got one bedroom."

"So what?" Sharon asked, then she suddenly realized what Julie was trying to say. "Oh I see. You mean you can't put me up as well?"

"Don't worry about it, Shah," Julie said quickly. "We'll all stay here until a bigger bungalow is available. It isn't the Centre's fault. Even though Colin told them that you would be with us there was nothing they could do about it. They haven't got a bigger bungalow vacant at the moment."

"Don't you even think of turning it down," Sharon chided her. "Colin would be far better off on the spot, and your place is with him."

"We won't leave you here on your own," Julie said stubbornly.

Sharon knew that Julie wanted to go to the Centre with Colin, but didn't like to leave her out of it. Suddenly she had a brainwave.

"As a matter of fact," she said brightly, "it might be better all round. I'm thinking of going into the interior to get a job."

Julie looked at her in astonishment. "You mean you want to go into the Outback? Whatever gave you an idea like that?"

"Well," Sharon answered slowly, "Pete has talked about it quite a lot and I am really fascinated by it. I thought if I got a job there, I could see it for myself."

Julie looked at her suspiciously. "Are you sure you haven't just thought of it, to make me feel better?"

Sharon laughed. "No way. As a matter of fact I was wondering how to tell you. I didn't want you to think I was fed up of being with you and Colin."

Julie's face cleared. "I wouldn't think that, and you know we love having you, but if that is what you want, we wouldn't dream of trying to stop you."

Sharon hugged her. "You are the best sister anyone could have, and I'm glad everything will work out well for all of us. You can go with Colin and you won't have to worry about me."

"You haven't got a job yet," Julie reminded her.

"No, but that's no problem. Pete says there is usually plenty of work around. A lot of people can't stand being cut off so much."

"Do you think you will?" Julie asked with a worried look on her face.

"If I can't, I'll head back this way and sleep in your bath, O.K.?"

Julie looked happier, and joined in Sharon's laughter. "O.K." she agreed. "Now, I must go and get changed and tell Colin the news. See you at dinner."

After Julie had left, Sharon sat on the side of her bed considering her situation. She couldn't make out why she had told Julie all that. It had been the first thing that had come into her head. It had worked though. Julie would move into the bungalow at the Centre quite happily now.

Immediately, the thought followed, why not do what she had said? Pete had made the Outback sound interesting. She really would get a job there. The idea was suddenly very appealing. She wasn't quite sure how to go about it. Pete would know though. She would ask him in the morning.

Over dinner, Sharon found she was being cross-examined by Colin over her decision to try for a job in the interior, but finally convinced him it was what she wanted. Then came the next problem.

"I'm going to one of the Aboriginal Reserves with Pete tomorrow," she announced casually. "We are going to stop overnight, to give us more chance to see everything."

Two astonished faces stared at her. "You don't mean that?" Julie said incredulously.

Sharon had to laugh at the dismay on her sister's face. Colin's wasn't much better.

"You'll trust yourself overnight with Pete?" he asked. "From what Jim told us, he has got quite a reputation with women."

"You don't have to worry on that score," Sharon replied easily. "Pete and I have got an-er-understanding."

Colin's eyes suddenly twinkled and he grinned. "You mean he has already tried to get you into bed with him and you told him what he could do?"

"Colin, really," Julie protested.

Sharon, however, only laughed. "Don't be daft Ju. Colin can speak his mind with me."

"I stand corrected," Julie replied primly, but couldn't keep a straight face.

"As to your question, Colin," Sharon continued, "It wasn't quite like that. Let's just say that we know where we stand with each other."

"Now we know why Sharon wants to go into the back of beyond," Colin quipped.

"I wonder what the Reserve will be like," Sharon said, changing the subject. It had just occurred to her that she would not only be somewhere near Pete in the Outback, but Nat also. It was a strangely disturbing thought.

Colin and Julie took the hint, but exchanged speaking glances. Both had come to the conclusion that Pete was the reason for Sharon's decision, and Sharon could almost hear their thoughts. She didn't enlighten them though, knowing it made them feel better about her going.

There seemed so much to talk about that it was late before they eventually made their way to their rooms. Sharon was tired, but found that sleep wasn't going to come as quickly as she had anticipated.

She tossed and turned in her comfortable bed, her mind in a turmoil. Was she right in moving to the Outback, nearer to the Westons' home? Would Pete think she was chasing after him, and she had just been playing hard to get today to keep him interested?

Would she get a job with accommodation thrown in, on one of the cattle stations, or in a town where

40

she would have the problem of finding somewhere to live?

The biggest question in her mind was, what would she make of it? The questions seemed endless, and she still hadn't found one answer by the time she eventually dropped off to sleep.

Even her sleep wasn't peaceful. First she dreamed she was being chased across a desert by a dark horseman, then she was lying in the shade of an odd-shaped tree and Pete was trying to make love to her. Suddenly it wasn't Pete holding her in his arms and kissing her, but Nat, his face dark and satanic.

When she awoke she felt really washed out and listless. She didn't know whether to put it down to the disturbed night or the unaccustomed heat.

It seemed too much of an effort to get out of bed, then she suddenly remembered she was meeting Pete early. She crawled out of bed, hoping a shower would make her feel better.

It must have done the trick because by the time she was dressed, with her hair brushed until it was shining and a light make-up applied, she was feeling more herself.

She had chosen brown flared slacks and fawn-checked cheese cloth shirt to wear. She didn't think she would need anything more formal.

Next, she put the few things she would need for the overnight stop in her vanity case, ready to just pick up when Pete arrived, then put everything else away so as to leave her room tidy.

She found she was a little late going down for breakfast, and Julie and Colin had already started eating.

"Morning everyone," she greeted them gaily.

"Morning, Shah," Julie replied.

"Hi there," Colin grinned. "How's my second best girl this morning?"

"Only second best?" Sharon returned promptly. "I'm disappointed."

Colin turned to Julie. "She must be all right. She's getting at me already."

"Serves you right," Julie answered unfeelingly.

Colin gave an exaggerated sigh. "Oh what an awful life I have," he complained. "Two women on at me. I don't know how I cope."

The girls laughed. They both knew he loved the bantering. The nonsense was so much a part of his personality. "Well, you'll only have to put up with one until tomorrow," Sharon comforted him.

Julie's face clouded. "Are you sure you are doing the right thing, Shah? You have only known him two minutes. How do you know he isn't planning on taking advantage of you when you're alone with him tonight. From what Jim said, Pete's girls don't often say no to an affair when he exerts his charms."

"Oh Ju, you sound like a Victorian father," Sharon laughed.

"So what?" Julie replied. "I feel responsible for you."

"Well, there's no need to, you know," Sharon assured her. "I'm a big girl now, and quite able to look after myself. I have been going out with men for a long time now, and haven't come to grief yet."

"Stop fussing Ju," Colin added his protest. "Now will you hurry up? I want to get started."

A few minutes later Colin and Julie left for the Research Centre, leaving Sharon to finish her breakfast in peace. Julie had insisted on giving her a final word of warning about going off with a strange man, much to Sharon's disgust. She found she was faintly irritated by her sister's well-meaning but unwanted advice, then her sense of humour got the better of her and she grinned to herself. I wonder what Ju would say if I got myself pregnant, she thought. She would probably take great delight in saying 'I told you so.'

"How long are you going to be?" a deep voice asked suddenly, startling Sharon out of her thoughts.

She looked up to see Nat standing by her chair. The colour rose in her face as she sat staring up at him.

"What's the matter with you?" Nat continued. "Anyone would think you had never seen me before."

"Wh-what are you doing here?" Sharon finally stammered. "Where's Pete?"

"Unfortunately, Pete is otherwise engaged," Nat drawled. "You'll have to put up with my company instead."

Sharon sat still for a moment feeling dumbfounded, then managed to pull herself together. "I don't have to put up with anybody's company unless I want to," she stated coldly.

A slight frown appeared on Nat's face, to be replaced by a bored expression. "Look, Sharon, I do not intend wasting a lot of time arguing with you. You want to see the Aboriginal Reserve, don't you?"

Sharon nodded, still bemused by the turn events had taken.

"Well then, be a good girl and fetch whatever things you think are necessary for your comfort, and then we'll be off," he told her.

Much to Sharon's amazement, she found herself meekly obeying Nat's command. She didn't want to go anywhere with Nat. She disliked him and didn't want his company, but still seemed incapable of saying no to him.

As she went upstairs to fetch her vanity case, Sharon couldn't help wondering what had come over her. Here she was, going off for the day, and night, with a man she didn't like. It didn't make sense.

Warning bells began ringing in her head. Thinking about stopping overnight, then remembering Nat's kisses, put her into a state of agitation. It was all very well going with Pete, she could cope with him, but she wasn't so sure about Nat.

Resolutely she pushed the thought away, deciding the best approach would be to take it as it came. With that firmly in mind she was able to view the trip with more favour.

She decided the best manner to adopt with Nat was cool friendliness. It was no good spoiling the trip by causing ill-feeling, so she banished her dislike to the back of her mind.

If Nat was curious about her change of attitude towards him when she joined him in the lobby a few minutes later, he gave no outward sign of it.

Four

"We are flying there?" Sharon asked in amazement.

"Sure. I am not going to waste time driving that far," Nat replied, grinning at the look of astonishment on Sharon's face.

"Pete never said anything about flying," Sharon told him.

"You would certainly have driven with him, that's why," Nat replied. "Pete hasn't got a pilot's licence. Always said he would rather travel on the ground."

Sharon sat in silence for a few moments, staring unseeingly at the route they were taking to the airport. Life was a long list of surprises, she mused.

"Why couldn't Pete come?" she asked curiously.

"He was already committed to—er—someone else," he replied with a slight hesitation.

Sharon realized straight away what he meant and she laughed. "You mean he had already promised to take another girl out, who he had forgotten about when he arranged this trip with me?"

Nat glanced at her with raised eyebrows. "You don't seem to mind being stood up for someone else."

"Why should I be?" Sharon asked promptly. "Pete doesn't owe me any loyalty."

Nat seemed to be having great difficulty in understanding Sharon's attitude. "Are you always so casual about your men-friends?" he asked curiously.

"Of course. I expect I could be as possessive as any other woman, or man for that matter, if I had fallen in love. To be quite honest, I've never met any man who aroused in me the tendency to be jealous, so it doesn't bother me."

Goodness, Sharon thought. Whatever am I telling Nat about my love life for? She was too busy with her own thoughts to see the expression on Nat's face as he looked at her. She would have been very surprised had she seen it.

"Are you comfortable?" Nat asked.

They had arrived at the airport without mishap and now they were sitting in the plane.

Sharon nodded, not quite trusting her voice. Nat had just been leaning across her to check her seat belt, his face so close to hers that she had felt his breath fanning her cheek. Unaccountably, her body was suddenly playing strange tricks on her. A tingling had run right down her spine and she felt strangely out of breath. What was it that had had this peculiar effect on her?

Nat seemed oblivious to her discomfort, so

nothing of the inner turmoil she was experiencing was showing, she was pleased to notice.

"Right," he said briskly. He proceeded to go through the regulation instrument check on the small two-seater plane. Satisfied everything was in order he radioed the control tower for take-off clearance, then taxied down the runway.

Sharon held her breath as they prepared to leave the ground. She hated this part of any flight, and it seemed worse in this small plane. Nervously she gripped the edge of her seat.

"Nothing to be scared of, Sharon," Nat said quietly, and Sharon was surprised at the depth of understanding in his voice. She would have expected him to be intolerant of a show of weakness on her part.

She smiled shakily at him, then suddenly the plane rose smoothly into the air. All Sharon experienced was a slight sinking feeling in the bottom of her stomach, which went off almost immediately.

"O.K. now?" Nat asked in his usual tones.

"Yes thanks," Sharon replied. "Sorry to be such a fool."

"Don't think any more about it," Nat answered. "Actually, I'll let you into a secret. I feel just the same as you when I'm a passenger. I guess having to concentrate on getting the bird into the air makes you forget to be nervous."

Sharon was pleased to discover this, if in fact it was true and not that it was meant to put her at her ease, and she smiled at him happily. Perhaps I have misjudged him, she thought. Under the top layer of toughness and mockery there seems to be something entirely different. Suddenly she felt on top of the world, ready to enjoy herself.

She looked out at the fast receding city of Darwin, its white buildings sparkling in the sunshine and interspersed with the darker patches of the gardens, then that soon disappeared to be replaced by more fantastic scenery. Tropical jungle was broken up by wide shining rivers, and Nat explained that in this northernmost part of the Northern Territories there were also extensive swamps which could not be seen properly from the air.

"Rum Jungle has got one of the richest uranium mines in the world," he continued. "I expect your brother-in-law will be going there. That is part of his job, isn't it?"

Sharon nodded. "Yes I think so, but never mind him. Go on with what you were saying about the area."

Nat grinned at her eagerness, but obliged nevertheless. "The Manton Dam, which supplies the water to Darwin was built in the jungle too. There are a lot of beautiful places to see, Crater Lake, Butterfly Gorge, and Knuckey's Lagoon. Don't ask me how that got its name," he chuckled as Sharon laughed at the name Knuckey's Lagoon.

"It is all marvellous," Sharon sighed. "I hope I'll have the chance to visit most of those places. Now then, what about where we are going?"

"You don't want a companion, you want a guide book," Nat teased.

Sharon's face fell. "Oh I'm sorry. I didn't mean to be a nuisance. It is just that it is all so new to me and I am interested."

"I'm only joking," Nat explained, putting a large hand over Sharon's for a moment before returning it to the controls.

Sharon had to control a gasp. It had felt like an

electric shock running up her arm when Nat had
touched her. Unconsciously she put her other hand
over the one he had held, as if to hold that fleeting
moment a little longer.

Nat didn't seem to notice anything amiss and
began talking again, which gave Sharon time to
gather her wandering thoughts together again.

Nat's voice penetrated and she strove to concentrate on what he was saying.

"We are going to one of the hunting camps
actually. There are several around, all within about
one hundred and fifty miles of Darwin. There is
Muirella Park, Nourlangie, Collinda and Patonga.
I'm afraid we won't see a great deal in the short time
we'll be there, but it will give you some idea of what
it is like."

"I can't wait," Sharon said. "How long does it take
to get there?"

"About an hour or so," Nat replied. "These planes
are pretty nippy."

"Tell me some more then," Sharon asked.

"No way," Nat replied firmly. "I've done enough
talking. Now it's your turn. Tell me about yourself."

Sharon proceeded to tell him her life story, finding it easy to talk to him. She suddenly remembered
long forgotten incidents, making him laugh at
some of her exploits, both at school and at the
Library College.

"You have packed a lot into your short life," Nat
laughed. "How old are you, twenty?"

"Twenty-two," Sharon corrected him without a
trace of self-consciousness.

"I can give you ten years," he said. "You make me
feel old."

"Don't be silly," Sharon said without thinking. "You are not getting old. In fact you're . . ."

"I'm what?" Nat asked as she suddenly stopped, his eyes twinkling.

Sharon blushed, but fortunately for her she didn't have to explain that she was going to say handsome and virile, because they had reached their destination.

"Saved, this time," Nat laughed. "There will be another time though. Then you can explain."

Sharon didn't answer, pretending to be absorbed in the view beneath the plane.

They touched down with only a slight bump, then walked across to where a large man in khaki slacks and shirt with a wide-brimmed hat was stood talking to a group of Aborigines.

The man caught sight of them, then saying something to the other men, strode towards Nat and Sharon. His face was wreathed in smiles as he extended his hand to grasp Nat's.

"Nat, it's great to see you. It's about time you came out of your hole to visit us."

Nat laughed. "Time is money, and I can't spare it."

The man looked sideways at Sharon, his face split by a huge grin. "Would you get this guy? To hear him talk you'd think he hadn't got a cent, instead of owning one of the biggest cattle stations around."

Sharon joined in the laughter, then looked enquiringly at Nat. He took the hint.

"Sorry, honey. This is Brad Martin, one-time room-mate of mine at college, who makes his living pretending to run this camp. Brad, this is Sharon Maine, fresh out from England."

"Glad to meet you, Miss Maine, or can I call you Sharon?" Brad asked, holding his hand out.

50

Sharon found her own hand engulfed in Brad's huge one. "Please call me Sharon," she answered with a smile.

"What have you got for us, Brad?" Nat asked.

"A couple of nice cabins right next to one another," Brad answered. "As the tourist season hasn't started yet there is plenty of room. It wouldn't have been so easy in a couple of month's time."

"Thanks, sport," Nat said.

Sharon looked around her with interest as Brad escorted them to their cabins. The camp was far larger than she had expected, with lots of buildings of all sizes.

For all Brad's disclosure that the tourist season hadn't begun, there were plenty of people about. Most of the white men to be seen were dressed in the same way as Brad, but they were outnumbered by the Aborigines. She commented on this to Brad.

"Actually, you've dropped in lucky, Sharon," he explained. "The Abos are gathered for a corroboree. Sort of impromptu dance," he added at Sharon's puzzled look.

"You'll enjoy that, Sharon," Nat said. "It's all very primitive, but you can't help getting involved in it."

"All the neighbouring tribes have been coming in for a few days now," Brad continued. "It's only occasionally that this happens, so you couldn't have come at a better time."

"Is it to celebrate something special, do you know?" Sharon asked.

"Who knows." Brad shrugged his shoulders. "Perhaps they are celebrating the end of the 'wet season,' or it could be something to do with 'Dream Time,' their story of creation."

"I don't think anybody really understands the Aborigine," Nat added. "They are a very close people, with secrets handed down for generations. All of a sudden the urge will take them to leave their jobs and they will go 'Walkabout.' They will go suddenly, without any warning, be away for a while, then come back again and carry on as if nothing had happened."

"That must make it difficult for their bosses," Sharon laughed. "Fancy your work force suddenly disappearing."

"Fortunately our white stockmen don't do the same," Nat replied, adding with a grin, "except when they get drunk."

By this time the trio had reached the cabins. Nat followed Sharon into hers and put her case down. "If you need anything, just call," he said. "I'm only a few feet away."

Sharon smiled. "Thanks, Nat."

"I'll give you a few minutes to get settled in, then I'll give you a call. We'll have a look round the camp, then get something to eat. We can go further afield this afternoon.

"All right," Sharon agreed, thinking nothing of falling in with his plans so easily.

Left alone, Sharon wandered round the cabin. It was small, but well appointed. It consisted of living-room, bedroom, shower unit and toilet, and a small room for making a hot drink or light snack.

The living-room was sparsely furnished, with wooden table and chairs, a sofa and a sort of Welsh dresser. The wooden floor was covered with woven rush mats, each with different patterns in vivid colours. Sharon knew that the Aborigines were good craftsmen and wondered if they had made the mats.

Sharon carried her case through to the bedroom, putting it onto one of the twin beds. In here as well, the furnishings were simple. A chest of drawers and single wardrobe stood against the walls, and once again rush mats covered the floor. The twin beds were already made up, their matching bedspreads woven in a patchwork design.

Sharon opened her case and carried her toilet articles through to the shower cubicle. A white wash basin stood in the corner with a shelf and small mirror above it. She arranged her things on the shelf, hanging her towel on the rail. She then splashed her face with cold water and re-applied her light make-up. A comb flicked through her long hair completed her efforts and she was ready for when Nat called her.

A couple of minutes later, the knock came on the door and she hurried to answer it.

Nat seemed taken aback by the brilliant smile of greeting he received, but all he said was, "Ready?"

They strolled round the cabins, Sharon noting that all the doors and windows were screened for protection against insects. On the verandas of each cabin, loungers and low tables were placed for anyone wanting to sit outside.

To the one side of the camp were the storage huts and in the middle stood the communal dining-hall and cookhouse. Not far away, on the outer edge of the camp was a bungalow, taking up about twice as much space as the cabins, one side with the notice OFFICE above the door.

"As you might have guessed, this is where Brad

lives," Nat said. "He has asked us in for a drink before lunch. I hope you don't mind."

"Not at all," Sharon replied. "I liked him straight away."

"Not too much, I hope," Nat told her.

Sharon raised enquiring eyebrows at him. "He is already spoken for," he explained. "He is getting married in a couple of weeks time, before the busy season starts."

"Oh, I see," Sharon replied quietly, feeling a little disappointed that that was the only reason Nat had for his remark, but not knowing quite why she should feel that way.

Nat knocked on the office door, but it was from another door further along the veranda that Brad called to them. "Come in here. The office I only use for official business. The trouble with living on the job is it's difficult to keep your official and private lives apart."

They followed him into a spacious living-room. There were far more home comforts than in the cabins, but that was only to be expected, Sharon thought, her gaze taking in the deep armchairs and sofa. Bright covers adorned them and there were also a lot of scatter cushions. A woman's touch, she decided. A man would have more utility furniture.

A fluffy rug lay in front of an imitation fireplace holding an electric fire. A table and four chairs stood under long windows, looking out away from the camp towards a clump of trees and grassland covered with a profusion of spiky bushes.

Alongside the fireplace was a large bookcase, all the shelves full with everything from encyclopedias to up-to-date paperbacks. Along one wall was a sideboard, and next to it was a low table with a stereo unit on it. Everywhere was spotlessly clean, with the furniture highly polished.

"Oh, I'm sorry," she started guiltily as Nat touched her arm. "I didn't mean to appear nosey."

"Don't worry about it," Brad grinned. "Do you like my humble abode?"

"Yes I do," Sharon told him sincerely. "Do you do your own housework?"

"Not me," he replied with a laugh. "I'm hopeless on the domestic scene. A couple of Aboriginal girls usually clean for me. Mind you, they are a bit slack at times. It's looking good at the moment because Sue has been here for a few days."

"Is Sue your fiancée?" Sharon asked.

"Yes. Prettiest little girl you ever did see, present company excepted," he added gallantly.

Sharon laughed. "You won't know yourself with a wife around."

"She's a proper homemaker," Brad told them proudly. "She came here armed with new covers and curtains and I don't know what else. I thought I was in the wrong place by the time she had finished."

"That's the sort of woman to have," Nat said. "Never mind all this Women's Lib thing. The ideal woman is someone who will look after the running of the house and raising a family, and keeping her man happy."

Sharon looked at him indignantly. "Male chauvinist pig," she muttered.

Nat raised his eyebrows but Brad guffawed loudly. "Take no notice of what Nat said, Sharon. If he married a meek little woman he would be bored to death with her after a few weeks, after the usual er-

basic attraction wore off and there was nothing else left."

Sharon blushed at the implication, but this time it was Nat who laughed out loud. "You know me well, mate," he told Brad, "but as I'm not the marrying kind it doesn't arise," he added, and Sharon missed the sideways glance he gave her.

"Now then, what will you have to drink, Sharon?" Brad asked, going over to the sideboard which turned out to be a drinks cabinet.

"Just a fruit juice if I may, please," she replied.

Brad brought her a long glass of lemonade and put it on the low table by the sofa. "Hang on a minute and I'll get some ice for you. Beer for you, Nat?" he called back as he went into the kitchen.

"Thanks, Brad," Nat called back.

Brad came back with a tray containing two cans of beer and a bowl of ice cubes. He dropped a couple of chunks of ice in Sharon's glass then handed Nat one of the cans of beer, opening the other one for himself.

"What are you doing here with Nat?" Brad asked Sharon. "He doesn't usually bring a woman with him when he comes visiting."

Sharon knew Brad wasn't being nosey. It was a purely friendly question. "Well actually, I think he was rather forced into it," she replied with a smile. "Pete was going to bring me, then he got sort of sidetracked, so Nat brought me instead."

"Nat can't be forced into anything," Brad assured her. "If he hadn't wanted to bring you, he wouldn't have done it. Isn't that right, Nat?"

"I don't like to see little girls disappointed," Nat drawled, neatly evading the question.

Sharon felt the colour come into her face, angry at

Nat's tone. Little girl indeed! Anyone would think I was five years old, she thought angrily.

Brad was quick to sense the change in the atmosphere, and could have kicked himself for unwittingly being the cause of it. Somehow he had backed Nat into a corner, and Sharon had borne the brunt of his retaliation. Quickly he drained his beer, thinking there was more to this situation than met the eye. "If you're ready then, we'll go and eat. It isn't anything fancy, but it fills the gap."

Lunch turned out to be a strained affair, with Sharon still smarting under Nat's remark. She concentrated on her food, leaving the men to talk amongst themselves.

Brad left them immediately after he had finished eating and Sharon and Nat walked back towards the cabins in silence. Nat suddenly slipped an arm round her. "Still mad at me, honey?" he mocked. "You've got to learn to take the rough with the smooth you know. It's all part of growing up."

Sharon shrugged his arm off, but didn't say anything. There he goes again, she fumed silently.

"We'll go and take a look at the Aboriginal cave paintings this afternoon," he added as if nothing was wrong, but Sharon decided otherwise.

"No thanks," she replied coldly. "You don't want to be bothered with a little girl like me. I think I'll have a lie down instead."

With that, she flounced up the steps of the cabin and slammed the door behind her. She thought she heard Nat calling her, but didn't take any notice.

She half expected him to come after her but he didn't, and a couple of minutes later she looked through the window to see him striding towards Brad's bungalow.

She sighed and wondered if she had been right after all. She couldn't understand why she was so prickly where Nat was concerned.

Should I go after him, she thought, then immediately vetoed the idea. He was too arrogant already, and she wasn't going to make it any worse by running after him. If he wants my company, he'll have to run after me, she finally decided.

She sat on her bed, wondering what to do with her afternoon. She thought of all the books on Brad's shelves and wished she could go and borrow one, but Nat had gone that way so she couldn't go too.

She decided she might as well have a lie down after all, so she drew the curtains, then slipped off her slacks and top and lay on the bed in her bra and pants. She didn't really expect to sleep, but there was nothing else to do. She sighed deeply, and closed her eyes. What a trip this is turning out to be, she thought wryly. She might as well have stayed with Julie and Colin. At least she would have had someone to talk to.

Five

Sharon awoke with the strangest feeling that she was in danger. She wasn't sure if she had been dreaming, or it was a reality. She lay still for a few moments with her eyes closed, and began to relax.

Suddenly, a slight movement close to her made her eyes fly open. In the dimness of the room the tall figure of a man loomed over her, and she opened her mouth to scream.

A hand was put quickly over her mouth as the weight of the man's body landed on the bed beside her.

"It's all right honey, it's only me, Nat," the deep voice told her quietly, and he took his hand away from her mouth.

Some of the fear went out from Sharon's eyes, but she began to shake as reaction to the fright began to set in.

Nat muttered something under his breath and gathered her into his arms. "I'm sorry, honey," he said into her hair. "I didn't mean to frighten you. I couldn't make you hear when I called, so I came in to make sure you were all right."

Sharon rested in his arms until the shaking gradually stopped. She felt safe and secure, and perfectly at home against Nat's chest, with his arms locked tightly around her.

Gradually, her senses returned to normal and she suddenly realized that she was practically naked, the wisps of nylon which constituted her bra and pants not hiding anything. She was glad the room was quite dim, so Nat could not see too well.

She tried to pull away from Nat's restraining arms, but to her amazement, instead of releasing her he only tightened his grip.

"Nat, let me . . ." she began, looking up at him. She caught her breath at the look on his face. In his eyes she could see passion, but something else too, something elusive which she couldn't identify.

"Sharon," he murmured, and then he was suddenly kissing her with a passion which Sharon had never experienced before. Her lips parted involuntarily and the kiss altered, becoming more demanding as Nat felt her response.

After that, Sharon could not think, only feel. Nat pushed her back down onto the bed and stretched his long frame beside her. His mouth left hers to trail across her cheek and down her neck into her throat, then back to kiss her eyelids before once more taking possession of her lips.

Sharon's hands came up and pulled Nat's shirt out from his belt. She felt the muscles of his back ripple in response to her touch and she pulled him closer to her, willing him to go on with his love-making. His hand began caressing her body, across her bare stomach and coming to rest on her breast.

Even the wispy bra seemed an encumbrance, but Sharon made no protest when he undid it. She was past caring about anything but the pleasure of the moment. Her senses were reeling as wave after wave of exquisite feeling hit her body. She gasped as her breasts, free from their restraint, became the target for Nat's mouth. His tongue teased the nipples as they stood upright in her mounting passion.

She put both hands round his head, pressing him more closely to her. "Oh Nat, love me," she cried out, and the sound of her voice seemed to bring Nat to his senses. He suddenly pulled away from her to sit on the edge of the bed, his breathing heavy and ragged.

He ran his hands shakily through his hair. "Oh God," he muttered.

Sharon suddenly felt cold. "What's wrong, Nat?" she whispered.

"What's wrong?" he repeated harshly. "Do you realize what nearly happened? I could have taken you then with no trouble at all."

Sharon came back down from the dizzy heights she had reached with a bump, her face flaming as she realized that for the first time in her life she had come close to losing her virginity. The awful part of it was that she had wanted to. She grabbed for the bedspread to cover her exposed body, and Nat stood up.

"I'll leave you to get ready and I'll call for you in half an hour for dinner," he said, not looking at her. He turned as he reached the door. "I'm sorry, Sharon, I shouldn't have allowed that to happen."

Sharon lay huddled up in the bedspread for a few minutes after Nat had gone, her thoughts in a turmoil. Whatever must Nat think of me, she asked herself? Come to think of it, what did she think of herself? Suddenly, Pete's words came back to her, when she had told him she thought she was frigid. "You are a one-man girl. When you fall in love you will want him to touch you, and probably crave for more."

That was it then, she thought, her hands flying to her face in dismay. She was in love with Nat. The realization didn't bring her much joy though. Nat certainly didn't love her too. Oh yes, he had made love to her, but that didn't mean a thing to him. He had even apologized for doing it.

Standing under the shower a few minutes later, trying to cool her heated body, she still hadn't recovered from the shock of her discovery. How was she going to face Nat again, in the light of her new-found knowledge? At all costs, he mustn't discover her feelings for him.

She still hadn't made up her mind how to approach Nat by the time he arrived to collect her. This time she met him on the veranda, taking no chances. She held her breath, wondering what he was going to say, but she needn't have worried. He greeted her casually, as if nothing had happened between them.

"We're meeting Brad for dinner, then we will watch the corroboree," was all he said.

Sharon was surprised how calm her voice sounded when she replied, "I am really looking forward to that."

As they walked to the dining area, her thoughts took a complete turn about. She hadn't wanted to

mention the passionate interlude, but illogically she
was piqued that Nat could be so casual. She shook
herself mentally, resolving to forget it. Some hope of
that, a small voice in her head taunted.

Brad had said that the food wasn't anything
special, but Sharon couldn't see anything wrong
with it. Surprisingly she felt really hungry, and
waded through a huge steak and two vegetables,
followed by a thick wedge of apple pie and cream.
She even found room for some fresh fruit afterwards.

Brad had dug out a bottle of wine, and they
finished the whole bottle between the three of them.
When they had finished eating, Brad suggested they
go over to his bungalow for another drink before
going to watch the dancing.

The wine had already made Sharon's head slightly woozy, but she agreed to the suggestion whole-
heartedly. Nat gave her a strange look when she
asked for a gin and tonic, but said nothing. When
Sharon agreed to have another one however, he
murmured, "Will you be all right with that drink?"

"Of course I will," she told him gaily. "I'm not a
child you know."

"Don't I know it," he muttered, then took a huge
gulp of his beer.

The camp was deserted when they made their way
to the clearing where the corroboree was being held.
It seemed everyone had gone to see it.

Sharon had recklessly grabbed an arm of each of
the two men, and she danced along between them,
very gay and happy. The drink had gone to her head
a bit, so that her usual reserve was shattered and
her tongue loosened.

"It's lovely to have such handsome escorts, two no less," she announced, reaching up to kiss them both on the cheek.

"My pleasure, ma'am," Brad replied gallantly, adding, "If only my Sue could see me now."

Nat seemed strangely subdued and only muttered something incomprehensible. Sharon arched her eyebrows at him and tossed her head, then deliberately flirted with Brad. He took it all in good part, claiming to nobody in particular that he was enjoying his last bit of freedom before he was shackled to one woman for the rest of his life.

Sharon could see that Nat didn't like her behaviour with Brad, but some imp of mischief, awakened by the drinks, forced her to go on. She knew that Brad was taking it in the right way, and that really he had eyes for nobody but his Sue, but Nat didn't seem to understand. By the time they reached the clearing, he looked as if he was ready to commit murder. Somewhere in the recesses of her mind, Sharon knew she was only doing it to hold his attention, even if it was only anger she invoked.

Then she forgot both men as she took in the scene before her. The huge silver moon hanging in the dark velvet sky, surrounded by thousands of bright stars, illuminated the trees and bushes which formed the background to the clearing.

In the centre of a wide ring of spectators a huge campfire burnt, the smell of woodsmoke mingling with the other natural scents of the surrounding foliage.

On one side a group of ageing Aborigines sat, holding what looked like hollow sticks covered with strange carvings. Other Aborigines, vastly outnumbering the white people present, were sitting cross-legged on the ground, all staring towards the darker area outside the ring of light from the fire.

Suddenly there was a deathly hush, then out of the darkness about a dozen Aborigines leapt into the centre of the circle. Sharon gasped, taken by surprise, and unconsciously grabbed Nat's arm. She was so intent on the men that she didn't notice Nat's reaction to her touch.

The silence was broken when strange thumping sounds began coming from the men with the hollow sticks. Sharon looked over to see them blowing into the sticks. "What are those men playing?" she whispered.

"Didgeridoos," Nat explained. "They are ancient musical instruments."

"Funny things, aren't they?" Sharon murmured, then that was the last thing she said for a long time. The dancers began moving round the campfire, in complete accord with the beat of the didgeridoos and the hand-clapping which the watching tribesmen had started up.

Sharon watched intently, fascinated by the spectacle. Her whole attention was centred on the gyrating figures in the centre. The dancers, clad only in loin cloths, spun and jumped, waving their arms about. They started quite slowly, then built up to a whirling frenzy, seeming almost to go into a trance. Still they were in perfect time with the beat of the didgeridoos and the clapping hands.

Sharon could feel the insidious beat penetrating her mind and body, and was as excited as the Aborigines. If she had been able to take her eyes off the dancers she would have seen that everyone else was feeling the same.

The perspiration stood out on the dancers' exposed skin, glistening in the firelight, the elaborate coloured patterns painted on their bodies forming weird pictures as they moved.

Suddenly they stopped and dropped to the ground. Total silence greeted their performance, everyone bemused by the spectacle they had just witnessed, then the clapping and cheering began, echoing through the darkness. Sharon clapped and cheered as enthusiastically as anyone.

The dancers got to their feet and stood a few moments, their chests heaving in an effort to get their breath back, then they disappeared back into the darkness.

Sharon turned shining eyes up to Nat, her face alight with excitement and pleasure. "Wasn't that absolutely marvellous?" she cried. "If I live to be a hundred I don't think I'll ever forget it. I just can't find words to explain how it made me feel."

Nat smiled at her enthusiasm. "I have seen a good many such dancers," he told her, "but each time I enjoy it as much as the first time."

"Will they dance some more?" she asked eagerly.

It was Brad who answered. "That was really put on for us white people, although once they get started they forget everything. They will really expect us to go now, and then they will start again, with everyone joining in. I don't think they would mind if we stayed, but it might spoil it for them."

As they walked away, Sharon looked back to see only a mass of black bodies. More wood was being piled on the campfire, sending sparks shooting high into the air, reminding her of a firework display.

They walked back to the camp in silence, each

occupied with their own thoughts. The experience had sobered Sharon, and all the gaiety and sparkle had deserted her, leaving her feeling very tired.

Brad left them with a quiet goodnight, then Sharon and Nat continued on towards their cabins. Nat went in with Sharon, putting her light on and checking everything was all right.

"Do you want a warm drink before you turn in?" he asked, but Sharon shook her head.

"No thanks, Nat," she replied. "I'll get a drink of water, then I'm going to bed. I feel absolutely shattered."

"That dancing always makes one feel like that, drained," he explained. "Well, if you are sure you are all right, I'll be off."

"Yes, thank you, Nat," Sharon replied, trying in vain to cover up a huge yawn.

Nat stepped towards her, then changed his mind. "Goodnight Sharon. Sleep well."

"I will," she replied. "Goodnight Nat."

Sharon was too tired to do more than brush her teeth and wash her face before slipping into her cotton nightdress and climbing into bed. She fell asleep almost as soon as her head touched the pillow, then heard no more until morning.

She had a slight headache when she awoke, which she attributed to the mixture of wine and gin she had drank the night before. She took two of the pain killers she always carried with her, and by the time she had showered and dressed it had disappeared.

There was no sign of Nat, so she knocked on the door of his cabin. She couldn't get any reply, but refrained from going inside to look for him, wriggling inwardly at the thought of what had happened when Nat had done that to her.

Instead she strolled over to the dining area, thinking he might have gone on ahead of her. He was nowhere to be seen however, or Brad either, so she ordered some coffee and sat down to drink it in solitude. Not long after, Nat and Brad came in together, talking nineteen to the dozen. Brad spotted Sharon first and broke off the conversation to call good morning to her.

"Morning, Brad, morning Nat," she replied cheerfully. The men fetched their mugs of coffee and joined her at the table.

"Where have you been?" she asked. "I was beginning to think I had been deserted."

"No way," Brad laughed. "Actually, we've been down to the river to see if any of the animals were about."

"Oh, you should have woke me to come with you," Sharon told them in disappointed tones. "I would have liked to have seen them too. What was there, by the way?"

"Nothing much really," Brad replied. "There was only a couple of buffalo down at the water, apart from the crocs."

"We saw a whistle duck and one or two pied geese on the way," Nat added, "and heard a boar snuffling about in the undergrowth, but that's all."

"Are there many wild animals and birds around here?" Sharon asked.

"Definitely," Brad replied. "You see, the area is virtually untouched by man, so therefore there is a near perfect balance of nature."

"The growth and conditions are so good," Nat

added, "and it is the natural habitat for so many things."

"Like what?" Sharon prompted, genuinely interested in all aspects of nature.

"The list is almost endless. There is plenty of game such as boar, geese, kangaroo bird, ducks, teal, quail, etc.," Brad reeled off. "If it is only for looking and not eating, there are several varieties of parrot, all brilliantly coloured, then there are budgerigars, finches, eagles, emus and the dancing brolga. If you wanted to get a look at all these you should come on one of our wild-life tours during the season. The guides know the best places to find everything, and they are really helpful."

Nat grinned. "I think Sharon can do without all your sales talk Brad. You sound like a guide book."

Brad laughed. "I'm not surprised," he replied. "I learn them by heart, then I can reel them off to interested customers, making them think I know it all."

"I don't care if you did learn it from a book, which I doubt anyway," Sharon declared. "You have sold it to me, and all being well I'll be back later in the year to see for myself."

"I hope you will. Maybe you can come as our guest and stop with us. I'm sure Sue will be glad to have you."

"That's very kind of you Brad," Sharon smiled, privately thinking that men could be pretty insensitive. A newly married girl wouldn't want to share her home and husband with another woman.

Brad turned to Nat. "What time have you got to get away today?"

"Before lunch, I'm afraid. I've got a conference

with some guys from one of the Agricultural Research Centres. Something about new ideas on cattle feeding," he explained.

"Oh, does that mean we won't have time to see anything else?" Sharon complained.

"Sorry, it does." Nat grinned suddenly. "If you hadn't slept all afternoon yesterday, we could have seen more."

Sharon went red, ashamed of her childish behaviour in walking out on him, but said valiantly, "That was your fault."

Brad looked from one to the other, noticing Sharon's high colour and Nat's mocking expression, and decided to change the subject. "Why don't you take Sharon to the shop, Nat? Perhaps she can find something to take back with her."

"Oh yes," Sharon agreed, smiling again.

Sharon spent a happy half an hour in the shop which housed native crafts. Nat watched her indulgently as she went from one thing to another, exclaiming at the workmanship.

In the end she close a pandamus mat for Julie to put in the bungalow, and a native spear for Colin, choosing a richly decorated basket for herself. She objected when Nat offered to buy them for her, so in the end they reached a compromise. Sharon paid for the presents for Julie and Colin, and Nat bought the basket for her.

Nat looked at his watch. "Well, I'm afraid that's about all the time we have got left," he told Sharon.

She sighed. She liked being here with Nat, wishing they didn't have to go back so soon. When Nat got back to Darwin he wouldn't bother with her any more, she felt sure.

It had been an interlude he had more or less been

forced into, and even if he had taken advantage of the situation once, it hadn't really meant anything to him. It had been a shocking revelation to her, but only an automatic reaction for Nat. How many men, finding a near naked girl in his arms, wouldn't have done exactly the same?

"Is your case ready?" Nat interrupted Sharon's thoughts.

"Oh—oh yes," she replied. "I've left it just inside the door."

"Right then, we'll go and collect it, then say goodbye to Brad."

Brad accompanied them to the airstrip. Nat put everything into the plane then climbed down again to shake Brad's hand, telling him to bring Sue down to Weston Downs as soon as he could.

"I'll do that," Brad promised. "I won't be able to get away until towards the end of the year, but there is nothing stopping you visiting here again. Make sure you bring Sharon with you again."

"We'll wait and see how it goes, mate," Nat replied noncommittally. He turned to Sharon. "Come on then. Let's get started."

Sharon held out her hand to Brad, who grasped it warmly, then bent down to kiss her cheek.

"Oh thank you, kind sir," she quipped, to cover her embarrassment.

Brad laughed. "My pleasure, ma'am. Now don't forget to come back soon."

"I won't," Sharon promised, then, with Nat's assistance, climbed into the plane. The feel of his hands around her waist as he helped her up sent shivers of delight up and down her spine, and she stepped quickly inside, anxious to move away in case he felt her reaction.

Nat climbed in after her. Sharon tensed in anticipation of his closeness when he checked her seat belt, and didn't know whether to be glad or sorry when he just looked over, saying casually, "Seat belt O.K.?"

Sharon nodded, relaxing. "Yes, thanks," she replied.

Once again, Nat was meticulous in his safety checks, but shortly, after a final wave to Brad, they were airborne. Sharon was so busy with her thoughts that she didn't have time to be nervous, and was surprised at how easy it was.

"No take-off nerves this time?" Nat asked with a grin.

"I must be getting used to it," she replied casually.

"You can get used to anything, in time," Nat commented.

Sharon was silent. She certainly hadn't got used to the idea of being in love with Nat. It would be easier if the feeling was mutual, but as it was, she would have to try to forget it.

The flight was uneventful, the time passing quickly. Conversation was desultory, neither of them feeling much inclined to talk. When they landed, Nat carried Sharon's things to the car, but still seemed strangely preoccupied.

Once or twice, Sharon was going to say something, but glancing over and seeing the frown on Nat's face, decided against it. She felt a little piqued that he seemed to have forgotten her, believing his thoughts were centred on the forthcoming conference. How wrong could she be?

"Do you mind if I drop you outside?" Nat roused himself sufficiently to ask as they neared the hotel.

Sharon replied, "No, that's all right. I know you are in a hurry."

Nat glanced at her quickly, suspecting sarcasm, but could detect none in Sharon's open smile. He smiled back, and Sharon's heart somersaulted. God, how handsome he is, she thought. They pulled up outside the hotel, and Nat signalled to a porter to fetch her things.

"What is your room number?" he asked her.

"Two-oh-four," Sharon replied.

Nat gave the number to the porter, together with a considerable tip. The man grinned appreciatively, gathering Sharon's things together with great enthusiasm.

Nat seemed anxious to get away. He opened the car door for Sharon to get out with a quick, "I'll be seeing you."

"Bye, Nat," Sharon replied. "Thank you for the trip. I really enjoyed it."

Nat's quick smile flashed out. "It was a break for me too," he answered.

Sharon stood on the pavement, watching until the car went out of sight, then with a sigh, turned and went slowly into the hotel.

Six

Sharon and Julie were sitting in Sharon's room. They were both ready to go down for dinner, but Julie had just popped in to find out how Sharon had got on at the Reserve.

They hadn't had the chance to talk before. Julie had spent the day at the Research Centre, re-arranging the bungalow to her liking. It was fully furnished, but Julie, with her knack of getting the best out of things, had moved all the furniture around before cleaning up.

The bungalow was ready for occupation now, but as their hotel expenses had been paid up until the end of the week, they had decided to stay on with Sharon for the few extra days.

Julie had put her head round Sharon's door earlier, just to say that she was going to shower and change, then she would come in for a chat. Sharon had guessed there would be an inquest on her trip, and she hadn't been wrong. As soon as Julie came back, she started.

"Did you enjoy yourself, Shah? What's it like? How was the journey? Did Pete behave himself?"

Sharon laughed, putting her hands to her head in mock dismay. "Hang on a minute, Ju," she protested. "One thing at a time. Now, let me see. Yes, I enjoyed myself. It was a great place. The flight was great, and I didn't go with Pete, I went with Nat," she replied breathlessly, counting the questions on her fingers.

"You went with *Nat*?" Julie exclaimed. "I've heard of a quick change, but that beats all."

"I didn't plan it that way, Ju," Sharon replied defensively.

"I didn't say that you did, Shah," her sister said. "But why did you go with Nat? What happened to Pete? Was he ill or something?"

"If you'll let me get a word in, I'll tell you," Sharon replied with a laugh.

Julie, fully aware of her tendency to talk too much, grinned sheepishly. "Sorry, Shah. Do go on. I can't wait to hear all about it."

Sharon proceeded to tell Julie about Pete being busy elsewhere, and Nat offering to take her instead, then described the flight, the camp, and Brad Martin.

She missed out the passionate interlude with Nat, deciding discretion was the best idea. Besides, she didn't want Julie to find out about her own response. Julie had a habit of worming things out of people. She had been worried about Pete seducing her, and Sharon was not about to let her find out that she had practically begged Nat to do just that, and it had only been his control which had prevented it happening.

The story took some time to tell, because Julie insisted on interrupting to ask questions, and it was only when Colin banged on the door demanding to know if his wife had forgotten his existence that she appeared satisfied.

It was a great relief to Sharon to be able to ask Colin in to give him his present. He was really pleased with the spear and gave her a smacking kiss when he thanked her.

"I'll put it on the wall over the bed in the bungalow," he told her enthusiastically. "If anyone breaks in I can jab them with it."

"And I can use it to get you out of bed in the mornings," Julie told him mischievously.

Colin grinned wickedly. "It would be better if you used it to keep me in bed. The consequences might be more interesting."

They all laughed and Julie stuck her tongue out at Colin. "You put me to the blush," she said demurely, her eyes twinkling.

Colin grabbed her and swung her round before kissing her. "Not you."

"No, not really," she laughingly agreed. "After being married to you for three years, nothing embarrasses me."

"You'll regret that remark later," he threatened.

"Promises, promises," was all Julie said.

Sharon looked at them affectionately. They were the ideal couple. Her thoughts began to stray to Nat, wondering what it would be like to have the right to behave with him as Colin and Julie did. Wouldn't it be marvellous to share his life, and his bed, she added, then pulled herself up short at her wanton thoughts.

Julie was pleased with her present too. She decided immediately where she was going to put it. Colin took the mat and the spear to their own room, then they all went down to dinner.

"Are you coming out to the Centre with us tomorrow Shah?" Julie asked as they were having their coffee. Talk had been non-stop during the meal, with discussions about Sharon's trip, the bungalow, and Colin's new job. He was really enthusiastic about it, and knew if he acquitted himself well during the following year, he could well be offered a permanent post. It was a big jump up the ladder of his profession, and he meant to grasp the opportunity with both hands.

"I'd love to," Sharon replied to Julie's question. "I have heard so much about it from you two though that I feel I know it already."

"No prior engagement with Nat?" Julie asked slyly.

Sharon couldn't control the blush which rose to her cheeks, but managed to reply calmly. "No, of course not. He only took me to the camp as a favour to Pete. He won't bother with me again."

A wistful note had crept into her voice which Julie was quick to notice, and she looked curiously at her sister, wondering if Sharon had told her everything about the trip. She wasn't really nosey, but she loved her and was concerned about her. If Sharon had problems, she would like to be able to help if possible.

"Hi, everybody," a cheerful voice called.

Pete came up to the table and draped an arm casually around Sharon's shoulders. She flashed him a brilliant smile, glad of the diversion. Pete was a little taken aback by the warmth of her welcome. He had wondered if she would be mad at him for letting her down.

"Won't you join us?" Colin asked. "Have some coffee."

"No thanks," Pete replied. "I just called in to see if Sharon was free to come out with me."

"I'd love to," Sharon said with a smile.

"Would you care to come as well?" Pete asked Colin and Julie.

"I don't think so, thanks," Julie replied. "I'm for an early night," she added, stifling a yawn.

"Yes please," Colin leered at her, his eyes twinkling.

"Colin, really," Julie protested, blushing slightly. "Whatever will Pete be thinking about us."

Pete laughed. "Don't mind me, ma'am. Live and let live, I say."

Julie threw him a grateful look, before telling Sharon she would see her in the morning.

"Where are we going Pete?" Sharon asked as they left the hotel.

"I thought we would go to the Ace Club, if that's O.K. with you," he replied.

"Lovely," Sharon agreed.

"Look Sharon, I'm sorry I couldn't make the trip. It really was unavoidable," Pete told her quickly.

"Yes, Nat told me," she replied.

"What did he tell you?" Pete asked suspiciously.

"Only that a certain lady had prior claims on you," she laughed.

"It was an old friend of the family, Sharon. I would have got out of it if I could." Pete sounded embarrassed, but Sharon soon put him at his ease.

"Don't worry about it. I'm not," she told him. "I'm not your keeper."

Pete relaxed. "Thanks Sharon. You're a real sport."

He threw a casual arm around her shoulders. "How did you get on with Nat? I must admit he surprised me by offering to take you instead."

Sharon was glad of the darkness which covered the blush which rose immediately to her cheeks. "It was very good of him to take the trouble," she said stiffly.

"It killed two birds with one stone really. It gave him a chance to see Brad too. He didn't try anything with you, did he?" Pete added with a laugh.

"No, of course not," Sharon replied quickly.

"Didn't really think he would," he told her. "It's not his style. He always lets the women do the running after him, instead of the other way round. Too busy running the station to chase women, he always says."

Sharon was pleased to hear that Nat didn't make a habit of making love to every girl he met, but her calm was soon shattered by Pete's next words.

"Of course, there is Miranda."

Sharon tensed. "Who's Miranda?" she asked as casually as possible.

"Miranda is the daughter of our nearest neighbour at McMillan Creek. She and Nat grew up together, and everyone has been expecting them to announce their engagement. I think Miranda would have married Nat years ago, but for some reason he has always held back."

Sharon listened with a sinking feeling in the bottom of her stomach. So Nat was practically engaged, was he. No wonder he had stopped himself making love to her. He must have been feeling guilty.

Her last hopes died. Thank goodness he didn't know how she felt about him. It would have been embarrassing for both of them.

"I expect he will capitulate soon though," Pete continued, unaware of Sharon's reaction. "He is not getting any younger, and he will certainly want a son or two to follow him."

"Yes of course," Sharon murmured. She shook herself mentally, deciding no good would come of moping about what might have been. She resolved to put it to the back of her mind and enjoy her evening with Pete, and enjoy it she did. Having no emotional involvement with him, she was able to relax.

They danced their way through the evening, only occasionally sitting out to get their breath back and get a drink.

"I'll never make it back to the hotel," Sharon laughed as they left the club. "My feet are killing me."

"Shall I carry you?" Pete joked.

"Fine sight that would make," Sharon replied. "I can just picture it, you staggering along with me in your arms, my legs swinging about in mid-air, kicking anybody walking past. They will think we are either drunk or insane."

They walked along the city streets, illuminated by the brilliant silver moon which hung low in the dark canopy of the sky, surrounded by a myriad of shining stars.

Sharon breathed deeply of the heady scent of the tropical flowers. "I love it here," she told Pete. "There is nothing like it in England to compare with the sights and sounds that you get here."

Love's Dream

"You haven't seen anything until you stand in the middle of the Outback," Pete said. "Mile upon mile of empty plains, it is a world apart."

That reminded Sharon of something. "I was serious about coming to work there Pete, and now it is doubly important. The bungalow which Julie and Colin have been allocated is too small to accommodate me as well. Can you tell me how I go about getting a job there?"

"Well, I suppose you can answer an advertisement in the paper," Pete replied, "or register with an agency. There is one in Darwin. We have been there to see about help ourselves. Apart from needing the ordinary secretarial help, my mother is compiling the history of the Outback. You know the sort thing, families who originally setted the area, etc.

"It sounds interesting," Sharon answered.

Pete suddenly stopped dead, then picked her up and swung her round. "I've got it honey," he cried. "You come and work for us. I'll be right on the spot to introduce you around and show you everything."

"You can't mean it," Sharon cried, her thoughts suddenly in a jumble. "Everybody would think you had brought me there for your own benefit."

"That's a point, I must admit," Pete answered thoughtfully. He considered for a moment, his brow furrowed in concentration. Suddenly he snapped his fingers. "I've got it. All you have to do is register at the agency and then mention that you had heard of this job. Because Nat has only just put in the application, there isn't much chance of it being filled already."

Sharon was silent, her mind in a whirl. Dare she do as Pete had suggested? What would Nat's reaction be? More important, could she cope with living in the same house as Nat without either giving her feelings away, or going mad with frustration?

"Well, Sharon, what do you say?" Pete asked eagerly.

"I don't know, Pete," she replied. "I don't like doing anything underhand."

"What is underhand about it? You can do the job, can't you?"

"Yes, of course I can," she replied.

"In that case, why hesitate? You need a job and we need help. Nobody need know about our own arrangement. As far as anyone else is concerned, it is just a coincidence."

"I can't decide now, Pete. Let me sleep on it, O.K.?"

"Fair enough. Don't leave it too long though, or it may be too late," Pete advised.

By this time they had reached the hotel, and Pete accompanied Sharon to her room.

"Thanks for a lovely evening, Pete," Sharon smiled. "And I'll let you know about the job soon."

"O.K. Goodnight honey. Sleep well." Pete lowered his head and kissed her gently on the mouth.

"You're a beaut, do you know that?" he asked. His eyes glinted with mischief. "I don't suppose you will take pity on a lonely guy and ask me in for a minute?"

"No I won't," Sharon laughed. "Behave yourself."

Pete grinned. "You sounded like a schoolteacher then. Can I be your private pupil?"

He went to put his arm round her, but Sharon pushed him away with a laugh. She wasn't a bit worried by his teasing, because they knew exactly how they stood with each other. "You don't need to be taught anything," she told him. "Goodnight, Pete."

Pete pulled a face and sighed deeply. "Foiled again," he said. "My heart is in ruins."

"Goodnight, Pete," Sharon repeated.

Pete at last took the hint. "Goodnight, honey. Just one more kiss?"

"You don't give up easily do you?" Sharon laughed, then slipped into her room and locked the door.

All the time she was showering and preparing for bed, Sharon mulled the problem over. To go or not to go, that was the question. One part of her longed to go, to be near Nat, whatever the consequences, and the other part was scared to put it to the test.

The biggest problem was what Nat would say if she turned up on the doorstep to tell him s̶ coming to stay. Would he accept gracef̶ her to buzz off?

Her head had begun to ache, so tablets and climbed wearily int̶ mixed up and tired to make the ̶ closed her eyes, hoping sleep would ̶ She would decide in the morning.

When she awoke, her mind turned immediately̶ Pete's proposition. She went over it again in her mind, weighing everything up. Eventually she decided she would try for the job. The chance to be close to Nat was something she wasn't going to miss, whatever happened.

Also, Julie would feel happier if she knew her sister was settled in a job. She would be able to be with her husband without feeling guilty about leaving her on her own.

The decision finally made, Sharon felt as if a weight had been lifted from her shoulders. She jumped out of bed, eager to get along to the Agency as early as possible. Now she knew what she wanted, she was taking no chances of the job being snapped up before she got there.

She sang happily as she showered, then stood for a moment wondering what to wear. Trousers seemed to be out of the question for such an interview, yet she didn't want to be overdressed either. In the end she decided on a crisp cotton shirtwaister with a green pattern on a white background.

She was pleased when she surveyed herself in the mirror. She looked young and fresh in the dress, and she had clipped her hair back for neatness. White shoes and shoulder bag completed the en—— and she smiled at herself. Just right, she ——ht.

——e joined Julie and Colin for breakfast in high ——rits. Julie commented on this, adding, "Is all this ——citement at coming to the Centre, Shah, or have you discovered you have won a fortune?"

Sharon clapped her hand to her mouth and her face clouded over. "Oh Ju, I'm sorry. I forgot I was coming with you. I was going to the Agency to get a job. I want to get it settled as soon as possible."

"I thought it was too good to be true that you were all dressed up for my benefit," Colin said ruefully.

"Oh shut up," Julie told her spouse affectionately, then turned her attention to Sharon.

"If you are certain that is what you want, don't mind us," she said sincerely. "I must admit I would be glad to know you were settled."

"Thanks Ju. I knew you would understand,"

Sharon said gratefully. "I'm really looking forward to it."

"Well you know that if you don't like it, you can call on us and we'll work something out," Colin told her, serious for once.

"Thanks, Colin. I love you both. Now, I hope you don't mind if I leave you now. I am too excited to hang around here. I'll go for a walk until the Agency opens."

An hour later Sharon was sitting in the office at the Agency, talking to a friendly middle-aged woman who had introduced herself as Mrs. Carter.

"Now my dear," Mrs. Carter said. "First of all will you fill in this registration card, and then we'll have a chat."

Whilst Sharon filled in the form, Mrs. Carter busied herself with some letters, but stopped as soon as Sharon indicated she was ready. She studied the form for a few minutes whilst Sharon sat anxiously playing with the strap of her bag.

"You are very well qualified, my dear. You know you could get any job in one of the cities. What has made you decide on the Outback?"

Sharon was prepared for this question. "Well," she replied, "I have heard a lot about it since I have been here, and I'm fascinated by it. I can't afford to see it as a tourist, so to work there is the obvious solution."

Mrs. Carter nodded. "I see. Do you think you will cope with being so cut off, and what about the heat? Coming out so recently from England, you won't really be acclimatized."

Sharon smiled. "I revel in the heat, Mrs. Carter, and I have never been one for a lot of socializing."

"There is quite a bit of social life there," Mrs.

Carter explained, "but it is mostly home-made entertainment. You can't just pop down the road to the theatre and shops you know."

"I realize that, and I'm quite prepared for it," Sharon assured her.

"I'm not really trying to put you off," Mrs. Carter smiled. "It is just that we have to be careful. With the time and distances involved, we have to be sure that anyone we send won't want to come back in a week. The station owners don't want to be bothered with changing staff all the time."

"I expect they have got too much to do," Sharon commented.

That seemed to clinch the matter. Mrs. Carter smiled. "You sound a very sensible young woman, Miss Maine, and I think I can fix you up."

Sharon heaved a sigh of relief. She hadn't realized how tensed up she had been, in case her application was refused. "Thank you very much," she said.

Now for the second hurdle, Sharon thought. Could she get the job she wanted? As it turned out, it was so easy that it could have been laughable.

"I think there is a position available at one of the large cattle stations that would make use of your considerable talents," Mrs. Carter said, going through her files. "Yes, here it is. As a matter of fact, this only came in this week."

She studied the card. "The name of the station is Weston Downs, and they require someone for general clerical duties who can also assist in compiling a history of the area. How would that suit you?"

Sharon was hard put not to jump into the air. She held her excitement in check, afraid that Mrs. Carter would get suspicious. She couldn't control the colour in her face or the sparkle in her eyes though.

Mrs. Carter noticed it, but evidently saw nothing amiss, because she only said, "I seem to have hit the jackpot first time. You look pleased."

Sharon forced herself to keep her voice calm as she replied, "It sounds just what I wanted, thank you."

"That is what I am here for," Mrs. Carter told her. She then proceeded to tell her the salary, which was far higher than Sharon had expected, then she explained she would live as family, so she wouldn't have to pay her keep either.

"Oh," Sharon said as a sudden thought struck her. "How do I get there?"

"No need for you to worry about that, my dear. Mr. Weston has arranged all that. I will let him know when you are travelling. You will fly down to Alice Springs, all expenses paid naturally. You will then be met there and fly on to Weston Downs in their own light aircraft."

After a few minutes conversation, Sharon left the Agency. She was so excited she wanted to tell the whole world. She had got the job, and best of all she had been offered it, and hadn't had to ask. That made it all above board, without a hint of subterfuge, and it made her feel marvellous.

Seven

Sharon's stomach was churning as the aircraft flew nearer to Alice Springs. Now the time had actually arrived, she was once again having doubts as to the wisdom of it all.

It was only four days since her interview at the Agency, and here she was, on her way already. It didn't seem possible. Her thoughts went back over those four days.

She didn't think she had come down to earth during that time. She had carried on normally, saying and doing the right things (at least she thought she had), whilst all the time part of her was riding on cloud nine, concentrating on the future. What fate had in store for her she didn't know, but she resolved to give it a helping hand if she could.

She hadn't seen Nat again, for which she was

thankful really. She would have felt obliged to tell him about getting the job, and she was scared. He could quite easily turn her down and go to see Mrs. Carter again. At least she stood a better chance once she had actually arrived at the station. It would be more of a problem for him then to get a replacement.

Pete had called to see her soon after she had arrived back at the hotel after her interview, to ask what she had decided to do. When Sharon had told him it was already settled, he had been really pleased.

"That's my girl," he told her with a grin, hugging her in spite of the interested onlookers.

"I'm really looking forward to showing you around," he continued. He issued a word of warning though. "Whatever you do, Sharon, don't let on to Nat that I knew beforehand. I am going to be as surprised as he will be when you turn up."

Sharon felt a bit uneasy at the deception, but reluctantly agreed. It would probably be easier that way.

Pete looked at his watch. "I can't stop now, honey. We are flying back to the station in a few minutes. I escaped from Nat for a short while, especially to see you."

"Don't get into any bother through me, Pete," Sharon begged him. "Get back to Nat."

"Sure thing," he replied with a grin. "See you at home soon."

Why couldn't I have fallen in love with Pete, she thought after he had rushed off? Everything is simple and uncomplicated with him.

During the afternoon, Mrs. Carter had sent round to the hotel her agency card and ticket to Alice Springs. A short covering note gave her the date and time of the flight, ending up by wishing her good luck. I'll need it, Sharon thought wryly.

When Julie and Colin arrived back from the Research Centre, Sharon was able to tell them everything was arranged. They were amazed at how quickly it had all been accomplished.

"It's incredible," Julie commented. "They don't give you much time to change your mind, do they?"

"It's much better this way," Sharon said. When she told them who she was actually going to work for, their mouths dropped open.

"At least you know them," Colin finally said. "That will be a big help to you."

"It seems more than a mere coincidence," Julie said suspiciously.

Sharon could feel herself blushing, but tried to explain. "So you see," she finished up, "although Pete told me about the job, I didn't ask for it. Mrs. Carter at the Agency offered it to me because I have got the right sort of qualifications."

Julie had to be satisfied with that. "I only hope you won't regret it," she said darkly.

"Give over, Ju," Colin said. "It's Sharon's life. Anyway, what is wrong with her working for the Westons? Jim knows the family well, and likes and trusts them. That is good enough for me."

Julie uttered something which sounded remarkably like a snort, but said no more on the subject, much to Sharon's relief.

Sharon and Julie went on a shopping expedition the following day, supplementing Sharon's wardrobe with some jeans and lightweight cotton shirts and dresses. They also bought a large amount of things which Julie had thought necessary to add the finishing touches to the bungalow.

When Colin arrived back at the hotel in the evening, he couldn't believe his eyes. "Is there a shop left with any stock?" he asked his wife sarcastically.

Julie's eyes flashed. "You would be the first to complain if I had forgotten anything, so be quiet," she told him indignantly.

Colin only grinned. "I was just thinking about our bank balance. That is, if there is a balance after this."

"If that was the case, you would have to take a second job in order to put it back, wouldn't you?" Julie said sweetly.

"Oh what a terrible life I have," Colin mourned. "I'm only loved for my bank balance."

Julie hit him playfully. "Oh shut up. You don't know how well off you are."

The following days were spent mostly at the bungalow at the Research Centre. Sharon found the rest of the staff very friendly and easy-going. She noticed that Julie and Colin had fitted in tremendously well, already firm friends with the others. They would certainly have a good time during their stay, she mused.

The three of them had enjoyed a celebration at the hotel, their final evening together for a while. They had splashed out on champagne, and enjoyed an excellent meal. The time had passed quickly and it was very late when they eventually went to their rooms.

Sharon had been up early this morning, doing her final packing. There was only time for a quick breakfast, then Julie and Colin had accompanied her to the airport. Julie had been full of last-minute advice, so it was a relief to Sharon when she boarded the plane.

The voice telling all passengers to fasten their seat belts jerked Sharon back to the present. They were about to land. Her stomach felt upside down, and she fastened her seat belt with shaking hands. Then, with a slight bump, they were on the ground.

Sharon looked round nervously as she stood in the airport lounge a few minutes later, her suitcases at her feet. She knew she was being met, but not by whom. She hoped it would be Pete, but realized it was out of the question because he didn't hold a pilot's licence.

It seemed as if she had been waiting for an hour, but when she glanced at her watch she was surprised to find it had only been ten minutes. She was assailed by doubts. What if nobody came? Perhaps Mrs. Carter had got the dates mixed up and she would be stranded here.

It was only a couple of minutes later however that a familiar figure strode in through the door. Nat! Sharon's heart began thumping madly and her legs felt weak. Only five days without seeing him and now she felt like a man in a desert being presented with a glass of water. It was a few seconds before Nat spotted her and she had time to stare at him without his knowledge. Oh, how I love him, she thought.

Suddenly Nat caught sight of her and he stopped momentarily before striding towards her. "Sharon, what are you doing here?" he asked in amazement.

Sharon wondered if she had imagined that his face had lit up at the sight of her, because the look had gone by the time he reached her. All he was showing was complete astonishment.

Sharon didn't speak for a moment. Her mouth had suddenly gone dry. Now for the crunch, she thought. Wordlessly she pulled the card she had been given by Mrs. Carter out of her shoulder bag. On it was her name and registration number, and a notice to the effect that she had been sent by the Agency.

Nat studied it for a moment, and Sharon waited in an agony of suspense. What was his reaction going to be? The last thing she expected was for him to suddenly burst out laughing. Her eyes flashed indignantly.

"I can't see what is so funny," she said in a strained voice.

"It's too funny for words," Nat told her. "Talk about the long arm of coincidence. If it hadn't happened to me I wouldn't have believed it."

"Why not?" Sharon demanded. "It's simple. You wanted secretarial help and I was given the job. What more is there?"

"More than you know at the moment," Nat replied mysteriously. "I can't imagine Pete's reaction when you land at Weston Downs. He is forever singing your praises and complaining that I dragged him away from you."

Nat's voice had hardened, and Sharon was quick to notice it. She blushed, but managed to say calmly, "I really can't understand that. We hardly know each other."

"Perhaps from your point of view," Nat told her, "but I am not so sure about Pete. He is very impressionable when it comes to an attractive girl like you."

The implied compliment went over Sharon's head. "Oh don't be ridiculous," she snapped. "We don't feel anything for each other except friendship."

"You might only feel friendly, honey," Nat told her,

"but Pete has got it pretty bad over you. He'll get over it though."

Sharon had no time to ask what he meant by that last remark because Nat was talking again. "Well, it is no use standing here. We'd better make tracks for home. I haven't got all day."

He picked up her two suitcases and moved towards the door, leaving her to grab her vanity case and run after him. As she followed him to the waiting aircraft, the same one in which they had flown to the hunting camp, her heart began to sing. It was going to be all right. Nat didn't mind her being there.

She hadn't realized how scared she had been that he would turn her away. Now she felt all of a tremble as reaction set in. She was glad to take her seat in the plane.

"Are you O.K.?" Nat asked.

"Yes thanks," Sharon replied, none of the inward quivering showing in her voice. Sitting in such close proximity to Nat was doing strange things to her senses. It was all she could do to prevent herself from reaching out to touch him.

A few minutes later they were on their way. "How far is it to your station, Nat?" Sharon asked.

"About four hundred miles," he answered. "Our nearest township is Tennant Creek, although we don't have to make the trip very often. We are fairly self-sufficient, and most other things we need are air-lifted to us. The plane also brings in the mail."

"It must have been difficult for people living there before the advent of air travel," Sharon commented.

"You'll find out about that when you start on this history with my mother." Nat's voice softened as he mentioned his mother. "I am afraid most of the work will fall on you. Mother isn't too well, but won't do anything about it."

"Pete said something about that," Sharon said, suddenly remembering something she heard. 'Nat is hard on every body but his mother.'

"Who runs the station then?" she asked.

"I run the station," Nat replied, "but if you mean the homestead, Mother still keeps her hands on the reins. She has three lubras to help her."

"What are lubras?" Sharon asked.

"Aborigine girls," Nat replied. "They work well enough if someone keeps pushing them. They are a very happy people, but tend to have the attitude that tomorrow will always do."

"Why employ them then?" Sharon couldn't resist asking.

"They have a right to work," Nat said sharply. "Don't forget this was their land before we came on the scene."

Sharon flushed. "I'm sorry," she said stiffly. "I didn't mean to criticize."

"You can't be expected to understand," Nat said condescendingly. "If you are with us long enough though, we will educate you."

"Oh thank you, I can't wait," Sharon replied sarcastically.

Nat raised an eyebrow. "You have got a sharp tongue, haven't you? Never mind, we'll soon cure you."

Sharon didn't answer. She couldn't. She was afraid to open her mouth in case she said something she would regret later. How she hated him when he was being sarcastic. No you don't, a tiny voice inside her mind said. You might be angry, but you don't hate him.

Sharon stared unseeingly out of the window, her eyes bright with unshed tears. She wished she didn't love him, then his remarks would not have the power to hurt her.

Nat, sensing how upset she was, suddenly relented. He laid a hand on her knee, and Sharon jumped as if she had been burnt.

"I'm sorry, honey," Nat apologized quietly. "I hadn't any right to speak to you like that."

Sharon kept her head averted, not wanting him to see her tears. He was having none of that though. He caught hold of her chin, forcing her to look at him. He muttered an exclamation before leaning over to kiss her gently on the mouth.

The action took Sharon by surprise, so she had no chance of disguising her reaction to it. A shudder went through her body and she involuntarily leaned closer to him. He tensed, then his mouth came down again, and this time his kiss was far from gentle.

A change in the engine sound brought Nat to his senses, and with a muttered "Damn," he pulled away to take control of the plane again. He then pulled a lever. "Auto pilot," he explained, then made to take Sharon in his arms again.

"*No*", Sharon cried, realizing that she had to put a stop to it before she gave her feelings away completely. Nat belonged to Miranda.

Nat looked puzzled for a moment, then grinned. "Well I must admit the cockpit of the plane is not the easiest place to make love in, but it could prove interesting."

"It's got nothing to do with the plane," Sharon said stiffly.

"Why not then?" Nat asked, his grin fading.

"Because I don't want to," Sharon replied.

"You weren't saying no at the hunting camp," Nat said nastily.

Sharon felt herself going red, and turned away. There was no answer to that accusation, so she remained silent.

"Are you like this with all your men-friends?" Nat continued. "You must give them hell."

Sharon was angry now and she turned back, her eyes flashing fire. "You have got no right to criticize me. Your behaviour leaves much to be desired. What about Miranda?"

Nat jerked his head up. "What do you know about Miranda?"

"Only that you are practically engaged. Did you forget that when you wanted to make love to me?"

Nat's eyes darkened. "Pete has been talking too much. I must have a few words with him when we get back."

"You leave Pete out of this," Sharon cried. "It has got nothing to do with him."

"It has got far more than you understand," Nat said. "Now let's forget the whole thing. I'm sorry my love-making is suddenly proving distasteful to you."

"But it . . ." Sharon began, then pulled herself up short. She couldn't explain without admitting that she loved him, and that was the one thing she couldn't do. He had practically admitted his involvement with the unknown Miranda, and she had no intention of being just a bit of fun on the side.

The time dragged as the plane droned on in the bright sunshine. Looking out, Sharon saw mile upon mile of red plains stretched out beneath her, and in the distance, a range of mountains. She would have liked to have known what they were called, but couldn't bring herself to ask Nat. Each time she had risked a glance at him she had been waiting for his expression to lighten, but he was still frowning darkly, his mouth set in a tight line.

Oh dear, she thought. How different it could all have been. If he had been free she wouldn't have minded his love-making. In fact she would have welcomed it with open arms.

She knew that, given just a little encouragement, she would try to restore a semblance of friendliness, but as none was forthcoming, she would have to hold her tongue. She was wishing now that she hadn't come. It would have been better not to have seen Nat at all than put up with his current attitude.

She sighed. Life was going to be very difficult at the station if they were going to act like enemies. They couldn't live and work together in close proximity with this kind of atmosphere prevailing.

Nat must have been thinking much the same thing, much to her surprise, for he suddenly said, "You and I will have to agree to differ in our attitudes, but I will not have the routine of the homestead upset by it. My mother would be put out by any friction between us, and she is not strong enough to cope. I therefore suggest we stick strictly to business when we are alone. However, we shall be expected to be normally polite in our social life, so I must ask you to bury your dislike of me then."

"Very well," Sharon agreed coldly, but inwardly she was relieved. She wasn't too sure if she could successfully hide her love if he was too friendly when they were alone. A small kiss given out of kindness or a casual touch could well be her undoing.

She turned her attention back to the land they

were passing over. The scenery had changed some-what, with more vegetation and trees to be seen.

"We're coming up to the homestead now," Nat told her in his normal voice a short while later.

Sharon strained her eyes forward eagerly. Soon she would see Nat's home. As the plane went lower, she could see it plainly. There were so many build-ings that it looked like a small village. A large two-storied building in white stone with a veranda running right round it stood a little apart from the rest of the buildings and she guessed this was the actual Weston house.

Nat flew the plane over the homestead to get in line for the airstrip, which was a fair way from the main buildings. They were soon down on the ground and taxiing towards some wooden huts.

As Sharon climbed down from the plane a utility truck came tearing towards them, dust rising all around it. It stopped with a screech of brakes and Pete jumped out.

"Sharon," he shouted, "what are you doing here?"

He strode over to the plane to pick her up and whirl her around. "Remember what I said," he whispered urgently into her ear.

"Put me down, you idiot," Sharon laughed.

Mindful of Nat's watchful gaze, Pete continued, "I don't get it. Nat goes to fetch the new office help and comes back with you instead."

Following Pete's instructions, Sharon answered, "But I am the new office help. The Agency gave me the job and here I am."

"That's just great," Pete told her. "We'll have some great times together when I show you around."

"Sharon is here to work" Nat interrupted coldly, "not to keep you entertained."

Pete sobered a little, then grinned. "*Ah*, but she is entitled to some free time, isn't she?"

Nat didn't answer, but turned back into the plane to reach Sharon's luggage. "Make yourself useful and put these in the truck," he told Pete.

"Sure thing boss," Pete replied, catching the cases as Nat threw them down.

"Come on Sharon, let's get back to the house. Just wait till mother knows who you are. I have told her all about you."

Pete put Sharon's cases in the back of the truck and then helped her into the cab before climbing behind the wheel. She found herself wedged in the middle when Nat got in the other side.

She was very conscious of Nat's body as they sat there. His hard muscular thigh rested against hers and she was continually being thrown against his arm as the truck bounced along.

"Slow down, Pete," Nat demanded harshly. "You're not on a race track."

Pete obligingly obeyed, but it was to Sharon he apologized. "I forgot you aren't used to this kind of ride," he told her. His eyes glinted wickedly. "If it has made you sore at all, just tell me and I'll rub it better for you."

Sharon laughed. "Yes, all right."

"Cut it out, Pete," Nat said sharply, a frown marring his handsome face.

"O.K." Pete agreed easily, winking at Sharon. "Just trying to make Sharon feel at home."

"Making remarks like that is more likely to frighten her off," Nat replied.

"Oh no," Pete denied. "I can say what I like to you, can't I honey?" he asked Sharon audaciously.

Fortunately, Sharon didn't have to think up a

suitable answer to that one, for they had pulled up in front of the big house she had seen from the air and rightly guessed was to be her home in the immediate future.

As she was lifted down out of the truck by Pete, Nat already having entered the house, she looked around, wondering what sort of a time she was going to have as an employee of the wealthy Westons.

Eight

"Oh it's beautiful," Sharon said as she looked around the homestead. Its white facade shone in the sunshine. The veranda was covered in a mass of foliage. Pink and mauve bougainvillaeas climbed up the posts and onto the roof. The flower beds just outside were a riot of colour, full of blue plumbago and pink freesias, and even roses.

"It is my mother's pride and joy," Pete told her. "My father built this house especially for her, and laid the flower beds and lawn. The site of the original homestead is about a hundred yards over to the west. That one of course was mostly wood, but Dad made this one to last forever, he said."

"Pete, I think it would be good manners if you were to bring Sharon in to meet Mother," Nat's voice came sharply from the veranda.

"Yes of course," Pete replied, looking a bit

ashamed. "Come on, Sharon. You'll get on well with Mother, I'm sure."

"I hope so," Sharon murmured.

They entered a spacious hallway with several doors opening off it, and a wide carved staircase.

"Don't be scared," Pete whispered as he sensed her nervousness. "Mother is a darling."

Sharon didn't know what the mother of two large sons would look like, but she was totally unprepared for the delicate diminutive lady sitting in a chair by wide french windows. Pete took her arm and led her over to the window. "Mother, this is Sharon Maine."

Mrs. Weston smiled and held out her hand. "Welcome to Weston Downs, Miss Maine. Nat has been telling me you are the same Sharon whom Pete hasn't stopped talking about since he came back from Darwin."

"Yes, I am," Sharon blushingly agreed. "I wanted to see the Outback, and couldn't afford to tour it, so the only way was to get a job here. When Mrs. Carter at the Agency offered me this position, I couldn't believe it."

"What a coincidence," Mrs. Weston echoed Julie's words. "Did you tell her you knew my sons?"

Sharon hadn't been prepared for that question. "Er-no, I didn't," she admitted slowly.

"Good for you," Mrs. Weston said briskly, causing Sharon to stare at her. "It was none of her business."

Sharon didn't know what to make of this tiny lady. Lady she definitely is, she thought. Her short grey hair was beautifully styled in waves, and her dark blue dress well cut and obviously expensive.

Her thoughts were interrupted when Mrs. Weston began talking again. "Well I expect you are tired and hungry after all the travelling, my dear. If you would like to freshen up, I will arrange for something to eat for you."

She rang a tiny bell which was on a low table at her side. An Aborigine girl with a wide smile came bouncing into the room. "Yes, Mrs. Weston?" she asked politely.

"Show Miss Maine to her room please Nell, then come back here."

"O.K. Mrs. Weston." Nell turned to Sharon. "You come along with me, Missy?"

"Thank you," Sharon smiled, moving to follow the girl.

"I'll see you a little later, Miss Maine," Mrs. Weston called after her.

Sharon turned for a moment. "Yes. Thank you Mrs. Weston," she replied.

Nell led her up the beautiful staircase and along a landing. "You stay along here," she told her, opening a door at the far end.

Sharon found herself in a large airy room, with long wide windows. The room contained light oak furniture and a huge double bed with a brass bedstead. The floor was covered in green carpet and the curtains were patterned with yellow daisies and green leaves, on a white background. The bedspread matched the curtains and the effect of the whole room was "English Spring-time."

"You all right now?" Nell asked.

"Yes thank you," Sharon replied. "Oh, where's the bathroom?"

"Corridor over there," Nell explained, pointing towards the door.

She must mean opposite, Sharon thought. "Thank you. You had better go back to Mrs. Weston now, hadn't you?" she suggested. Nell nodded and danced away.

Sharon could see that her luggage had already been deposited at the foot of the bed, so she opened the one case to shake out a blue tricel sheath dress, which she knew wouldn't have creased. She then found her toilet bag and went to look for the bathroom.

She noticed there were two doors opposite hers, and wondered which one belonged to the bathroom. She stood undecided for a moment, then took the plunge. She opened the one nearest to her and stood just inside the door, rooted to the spot.

"Oh, I'm sorry," she stammered as her startled gaze met the dark eyes of Nat, standing by the bed clad in nothing but a pair of undershorts.

Nat raised his eyebrows. "Don't be sorry, honey. Come in and finish what you wouldn't in the plane. It's certainly more comfortable."

Sharon blushed a fiery red, but stood her ground bravely. "N—no thanks," she answered, her voice shaking slightly. "I—I was looking for the bathroom."

"Next door," Nat explained, "but you can stay here if you'd prefer."

"Oh you . . ." Sharon began, then backed out of the room, slamming the door behind her. Even through the door she could hear Nat's mocking laughter, and she covered her face with her hands. She began to shake. She wondered how Nat would have reacted if she had taken him up on his offer. He would never know how close she had been to doing just that.

The sight of his near naked body, the dark hairs

on his chest and the sun-tanned muscular arms and shoulders, had made her go weak at the knees. She sighed. If only there wasn't Miranda, she might risk a rebuff, but there was no way she was going to make a fool of herself for nothing.

Pulling herself together, she opened the door next to Nat's. To her relief she had got it right this time. She felt hot and sticky, and looked longingly at the shower unit in the corner. Knowing Mrs. Weston was having a meal prepared for her though, she reluctantly settled for a quick wash instead.

She looked round the bathroom. The light blue of the bathroom suite against the white tiled walls was very effective. The blue and white tiles on the floor, covered by a blue fluffy, rug, completed the picture of coolness.

Realizing she had wasted a lot of time, she hurried her wash and returned to her room, heaving a sigh of relief that there was no sign of Nat. She changed into the blue dress, pulled a comb through her hair and applied a dab of lipstick, then she was ready.

Pete met her in the hall, greeting her with a low whistle. "You look great, honey," he told her.

Sharon smiled. "Thanks. Where do I go, Pete? Your mother said she would arrange some food for me."

"In the dining-room, over there," he pointed. "Look, I'll see you later. I've got some work to do."

Sharon went into the room Pete had indicated. To her dismay, Nat was already sitting at the table. He looked up.

"Come and eat," he invited, acting as if the encounter of a few minutes earlier hadn't taken place.

"Thank you," Sharon replied stiffly, pulling out a chair opposite him.

Cold meat and salad had been set out, and a bowl of fresh fruit. Sharon helped herself to the meat and salad, and then concentrated fiercely on eating. She felt rather awkward, sitting alone with Nat. She thought she ought to speak, but could think of nothing to say.

It was Nat who spoke first. "You had better use the rest of the day to get settled in and find your way about," he told her.

"I can start straight away if you like," Sharon ventured.

"It doesn't matter," Nat replied. "We have been without help for a few weeks now. Another day won't make any difference."

Sharon felt rebuffed. She was only trying to be helpful, and all she got was her offer thrown back in her face. She looked down at her plate, willing herself not to glance at Nat to see what expression was on his face.

"Right, that does me," Nat said a few minutes later. "I've got some work to do. I'll take you to the office after dinner and show you what needs doing first in the morning."

Sharon jerked her head up. "Won't you be there tomorrow?" she asked involuntarily.

"No, I will be needed out on the run," he explained, adding mockingly, "You are capable of working alone, aren't you?"

Sharon flushed. "Yes of course, but don't forget this is all new to me."

"You'll soon pick it up," he said in a kinder tone as he strode to the door.

Sharon laid her knife and fork down, and absent-mindedly took an apple from the bowl. She just couldn't understand Nat's quick changes of mood, and wondered if she was going to cope all right.

"I hope you have had sufficient to eat, Miss Maine," Mrs. Weston's voice penetrated Sharon's thoughts, and she turned with a smile. "Yes thank you, Mrs. Weston," she replied, "and please call me Sharon."

"Thank you, my dear. Perhaps you would care to join me in my sitting-room and I can tell you a bit about the history of the area I am trying to complete."

"I'd like that," Sharon agreed eagerly. She already liked Mrs. Weston enormously, and looked forward to working with her.

They went upstairs together, then turned in the opposite direction to Sharon's room. They entered a large pleasant room. It was totally feminine, with chintzy curtains and covers on the chairs. A writing-desk stood by the windows which looked out over a lawn, kept green by a sprinkler and surrounded by flower borders.

On a sideboard along one wall were various ornaments, and all kinds of photographs.

"I am a compulsive hoarder of photographs," Mrs. Weston explained, catching the direction of Sharon's interested gaze.

On the wall above the mock fireplace was a portrait of a large handsome man, bearing a marked resemblance to Nat. The piercing dark eyes seemed to be able to see out of the canvas.

"Is that Mr. Weston?" Sharon asked.

"Yes, that is my husband," Mrs. Weston replied quietly. "He was killed in a plane crash eleven years ago," she continued, "and I still miss him so much."

Sharon felt as if she had been allowed a glimpse into the tiny woman's heart, and felt privileged. She choked back a lump which rose in her throat, looking with compassionate eyes at her, standing in front of the portrait of her beloved husband, her eyes bright with tears and suddenly looking tired.

"Are you all right Mrs. Weston," she enquired quietly.

Mrs. Weston made an effort to pull herself together and gave her a watery smile. "Yes, Sharon dear," she replied. "I'm sorry, I don't know what came over me."

She dabbed her eyes with a lacy handkerchief, then said in a brisker tone, "Now then, what shall we look at first?"

She walked over to a low table in front of the sofa, on which stood a pile of albums. "Would you like to have a look at my photographs, dear?"

"Yes, please," Sharon said quickly. "I love looking at photographs. Seen in the right sequence they can describe a family without words being necessary."

Mrs. Weston gave her an approving nod. "We think the same way, Sharon. I am going to enjoy your company."

Sharon smiled, then sat down on the sofa beside Mrs. Weston, who had already reached for the first album.

"These are the older ones," Mrs. Weston explained, showing her the faded brown pictures.

For Sharon, the present time and her problems faded as the past jumped up at her from out of the album. Men in stiff collars with plastered-down hair and moustaches, and women in long heavy dresses, their lined faces showing the hardships they faced came to life as Mrs. Weston explained who each one was.

There were photographs of the homestead as it used to be, a single-storey wooden building. There was no sign of the beautiful flower beds, and Mrs. Weston told Sharon proudly that it was she who had started the gardens when her husband Josh had built the new homestead.

She told her that she had come to Weston Downs as a fresh young bride, full of love for her big handsome husband, determined to do her best to help him build up the station.

"I was a city girl," Mrs. Weston explained as her eyes misted with remembrance. "I lived in Sydney, and Josh came to see my father on some business. We fell in love immediately, but it took a while before I could convince him that I could cope with life in the Outback as it was then. He said I wasn't strong enough."

"I can understand that," Sharon interrupted with a smile. "If you don't mind me saying so, you look as if you would blow away in a strong wind."

Mrs. Weston chuckled. "That is what everyone thought at first, but I am stronger than I look. You would be surprised at how strong-willed I can be when I want to. I let my sons bully and pamper me because they enjoy it, but even they can't make me do anything I don't want to."

Sharon remembered Pete saying that she refused to see a doctor. She knew what he meant now.

"Anyway," Mrs. Weston continued, "eventually, Josh agreed to marry me, and my father gave his permission without hesitation. I think he was glad to get rid of me, then he could concentrate on his favourite, my younger brother James."

Sharon detected the underlying sadness in Mrs. Weston's voice. Basking in her father's love all her life, she could well imagine how she would have felt if he hadn't wanted her, as it seemed with Mrs. Weston's father.

Mrs. Weston opened the second book. "These are all from when I was first married," she said.

The photographs showed her as a young woman. She was beautiful, her face radiating her happiness. The ones of Josh could well have been present-day photographs of Nat, except for the difference in clothes.

"We were married ten years before Nat was born," Mrs. Weston said. "I was beginning to feel hopelessly inadequate, unable to give Josh the sons he wanted, but Josh never gave up hope. He always said that if God was going to bless us with children, it would happen, and if not, we would still have each other."

Sharon envied her simple faith in the love between her and Josh. How she wished it could be that way between Nat and herself. Unconsciously she sighed.

"Are you tired, Sharon?" Mrs. Weston asked immediately. "It must be very boring for you, listening to me reminiscing."

"Oh no," Sharon denied quickly. "I am really interested. I was just wishing I could be as lucky as you have been with your Josh."

Mrs. Weston patted her hand. "I am sure you will be, my dear. You are a kind and decent girl, and I am sure love is waiting for you."

She really is the sweetest person, Sharon thought. It was amazing that with the difference in their ages and backgrounds, there still seemed to be an immediate friendship between them.

"I have talked so much I am really thirsty," Mrs. Weston said with a smile. "Would you pull that rope over there? It is a bell Nat fixed up for me to save me running downstairs if I wanted anything. You'll have some tea with me, won't you, my dear?"

"I'd love some," Sharon replied, picking up the next album.

"Ah, that is the one with the boys growing up," Mrs. Weston explained.

Both boys were depicted at all ages, but it was the ones of Nat which Sharon studied the most. Even at an early age he showed some of the arrogance which was a part of his make-up now.

"They were terrors when they were small," Mrs. Weston remembered. "It was always left to Nat though to pull Pete out of the scrapes he got into."

Nell came in answer to the bell, and a few minutes later came back with the tea Mrs. Weston had ordered. She had also brought some lovely scones and cakes which Sharon tucked into eagerly. She poured the tea for them both, then Mrs. Weston continued.

"Pete was always more happy-go-lucky than Nat. It was probably because from an early age Josh began grooming him to take over the station one day. It was almost as if he knew something was going to happen to him. Both the boys were at university when Josh died, but Nat left immediately to take over, and he has been running the station ever since."

That explains a lot, Sharon thought. Nat had all the responsibilities, whilst Pete had much more freedom. Nat really hadn't had the chance to develop the same extrovert personality as Pete.

Mrs. Weston suddenly smiled. "I have been dropping hints to the boys that it was time they settled down. I would like to be able to hold some grand-children before I go to join Josh."

"You have got plenty of time left to enjoy grand-children," Sharon assured her, but privately was doubtful. The dark shadows under her eyes and the tiredness indicated some kind of illness. She couldn't hazard a guess at what was wrong, but she resolved to help this lovely woman if she could.

They talked on for a long time, Nell fetching the tea tray almost without being noticed. Mrs. Weston talked for a while, then asked Sharon to tell her about her family and upbringing. It was only when the light began to fail that Mrs. Weston jumped up with a muttered exclamation.

"Oh, look at the time," she said. "I hope Minnie has remembered to start the dinner. She does tend to forget," she laughingly added. "She is a wonderful cook though, once she does get started."

"I'm sorry I took up so much of your time," Sharon said.

"It was my fault, not yours," Mrs. Weston assured her. "I have enjoyed every minute of it, and I should be thanking you for being so patient with my ramblings."

"I have loved it," Sharon replied promptly, then impulsively leaned forward to kiss Mrs. Weston on the cheek.

"I'll see you later," she added, aghast at her own temerity. To her relief though, Mrs. Weston seemed pleased by the gesture.

"Yes dear," she replied. "Come down to the lounge for a drink as soon as you are ready."

Mrs. Weston stared thoughtfully at the door after Sharon had left. Sharon would have been shocked if she would have heard her, speaking aloud to herself. "Never mind Miranda. That is definitely the girl for my Nat."

Nine

Sharon hoped she was on time, going downstairs. Mrs. Weston hadn't said what time dinner was, but had said as soon as she was ready she was to go down. She had quickly showered, then stood undecided about what to wear. She had no idea if they dressed for dinner, but felt reasonably sure that Mrs. Weston wouldn't like anything too informal.

She finally put on an orange cotton blouse and long black skirt. It certainly wouldn't do to appear too showy. She was pleased with her choice however when, just as she reached the top of the stairs, Mrs. Weston came out of her room in a long dress in soft grey crêpe.

"Shall we go down together?" Sharon asked brightly, then she realized something was wrong with Mrs. Weston. Picking up her long skirt, she raced to where she was standing, looking white and strained.

"Are you all right, Mrs. Weston?" she asked urgently. "Shall I call Nat?"

"No, don't do that. It will only worry him," Mrs. Weston answered breathlessly. "I will be all right in a minute. I often get these attacks if I rush around."

Sharon noticed the slight bluish tinge around her mouth and immediately thought of heart trouble. She was worried about her, and her face registered her concern. "Please let me fetch Nat," she begged.

Mrs. Weston showed something of the strength she had admitted to earlier on. "No," she said firmly, her voice stronger. "He has got enough to think about without worrying about me. Now promise me you won't say a word of this to either of the boys."

Sharon, knowing she was being weak but afraid of upsetting Mrs. Weston, in case it was her heart playing up, finally promised.

"Good. I know I can rely on you to keep your word," Mrs. Weston said. She was looking better now, with the blueness disappearing and some colour coming back into her cheeks.

She pulled herself away from Sharon's supporting arm and drew herself upright. "Let's go down, shall we? The boys will think we have got lost."

She was a bit shaky as they started down the landing, and Sharon watched her with anxious eyes. "Why don't you go and lie down for a while?" she suggested. "I will make some excuse to Nat and Pete."

"They would see through you straight away," Mrs. Weston replied. "If you will just give me your arm to go down the stairs, I will manage."

When they reached the hall, Mrs. Weston withdrew her arm and walked into the lounge with her head held high. Sharon marvelled at her will power as she watched her acting normally, without a hint of strain.

Nat and Pete had already had a drink, and Nat refilled their glasses after giving his mother and Sharon the dry sherry they had asked for.

Both men had changed and were wearing ties, although they weren't wearing jackets. Sharon studied them as they talked with their mother. Both bore a resemblance to their father, but Nat's was the stronger face.

She blushed when she realized Nat had caught her staring, lifting a mocking eyebrow at her, and she looked hastily away. The moment passed, then Pete came over to talk to her. He sprawled out next to her on the sofa, draping his free arm casually round the back of her, resting his fingers lightly on her shoulder.

"You look more beautiful every time I see you, honey," he told her.

"Flattery will get you everywhere," Sharon replied with a laugh, knowing nothing serious was meant.

Petes eyes glinted wickedly. "Is that a promise?" he asked, moving closer to her. "Your eyes are like stars . . ."

He was interrupted by Nell coming in to tell them dinner was ready. "Later," he promised as he got up. Sharon was surprised to find both Nat and Mrs. Weston watching them, frowning. Oh dear, she thought, I mustn't flirt with Pete.

"Will you give me your arm, Peter?" Mrs. Weston asked.

"Certainly, ma'am," Pete bowed. "What have I done now?" he asked with a laugh. "She only calls me that when she is cross with me," he explained to Sharon.

"Will you bring Sharon, Nat?" Mrs. Weston said as she took Pete's arm and went on ahead.

Sharon stood up. Nat offered her his arm and she reluctantly tucked her hand under it. Her heart gave the now familiar lurch as she came into contact with him and she resisted the urge to move closer to him.

"Don't encourage Pete in front of Mother," Nat whispered. "I could see she didn't like it and I won't have her upset."

"Why should she mind?" Sharon whispered back, keeping her anger in check.

"Because, whatever he might tell you, he is destined for someone else, and Mother knows it."

Sharon raised startled eyes to his. "That is the first I have heard about it," she told him.

"I'll tell you later," he said as they reached the dining-room. Mrs. Weston and Pete were already seated, and Nat held Sharon's chair for her before sitting down at the head of the table.

Sharon was glad to see that Mrs. Weston seemed happy again, and was telling the men that she and Sharon had spent all afternoon looking at photographs.

"You haven't roped her in already, have you?" Nat laughed. "I told her she needn't start work until tomorrow."

Mrs. Weston only smiled, but Sharon said indignantly. "I loved every minute of it. You can't call that work."

"Well said," Pete applauded.

"I standed corrected," Nat said mockingly.

"You were right, Nat," Mrs. Weston said, "but I am

so interested in the history that I can't wait to get it done properly."

"You supply me with the details and I'll soon collate them," Sharon told her confidently.

"The station work must come first, you know," Nat warned. Sharon threw him a look of dislike, wishing she could throw a plate at him.

"I know that, Nat," Mrs. Weston said patiently, "but I am sure Sharon will find some time to help me too."

"I wouldn't miss it," Sharon assured her with a smile.

"Leave some time for me too," Pete said, but Sharon ignored him, pretending not to hear. She was not going to upset Mrs. Weston again. Or Nat, a tiny voice inside her added.

As soon as the meal was finished, Nat stood up. "Get Nell to bring Sharon and me some coffee in the office, will you Mother? I'm just going to put her in the picture about the work."

"Don't be too long," Mrs. Weston told him. "I expect Sharon is tired."

"I thought you said Sharon wasn't starting work until tomorrow," Pete said in injured tones. "I haven't had a proper chance to talk to her yet."

"And you won't tonight either," Nat replied. "Come on Sharon, let's get on, then you can get your beauty sleep."

With a murmured "Excuse me," to Mrs. Weston, Sharon got up to follow Nat. He led the way across the hall and into the office.

Sharon's eyes widened when she followed Nat in. It was obvious that there had been no help for weeks, as Nat had told her earlier, for the room was in chaos.

The desk and dark green leather armchairs were covered with papers, and they had even been stacked on the shelves of the bookcase. The drawers of the filing cabinet wouldn't close. In fact the only clear place seemed to be the radio receiver in the corner.

Nat grinned sheepishly as he caught her look. "I'm afraid I am not very tidy," he said ruefully.

"I wouldn't have guessed that from this room," Sharon replied sarcastically.

Nat grinned, and Sharon's insides somersaulted. How different he was when he was being natural. She flashed him a brilliant smile, and something flashed momentarily into his eyes. Sharon wondered if she had imagined the look of admiration, which she had seen, because it had gone so quickly. Wishful thinking, she decided.

Nat's expression hardened. "First of all, let's get this thing about Pete straight. You have told me yourself that you aren't serious about him, so this shouldn't matter to you. He is, or was," he corrected himself, "engaged to a girl called Janie Dillman, the daughter of an old friend, who is a banker in Darwin."

Sharon had a sudden flash of insight. "That was the girl he was meeting when you took me to the camp instead?"

"Right. Well, Pete was young and unsettled, so after a few months Janie broke off the engagement, leaving him free until such time as he felt ready to settle down."

"I couldn't see me doing that," Sharon cried involuntarily. "I would have settled for a quick marriage instead."

"And maybe regretted it?" Nat asked. "Janie is some girl, and she realized he would not settle down properly with her until he'd had a fling." He frowned. "I am afraid it has been a very long fling. He has had plenty of girls and plenty of affairs, but always goes back to Janie."

"And she stands for that?" Sharon asked incredulously. "I certainly wouldn't be used like that. I would tell him where he could go."

"So would I," Nat agreed. "No woman would mess me about, but that is beside the point. Janie knows that Pete will eventually grow up, then he will be a good husband to her, and she loves him deeply. That is why she waits. Anyway, we had thought he was ready to stop all his nonsense and get married, then you came along. He went overboard for you, because you are so different."

"Oh, was that the only reason?" Sharon quipped before she could stop herself.

"Don't be flippant, Sharon," Nat ordered curtly.

"Sorry," Sharon apologized, knowing she had been in the wrong. "But look Nat, I have told him all I feel for him is friendship, and there can never be anything more between us."

"It hasn't sunk in then," Nat replied. "Try a bit harder, will you? Mother will feel better when he is settled with Janie."

Mention of his mother brought a frown to Sharon's face. She forgot all about Pete for the moment, wondering how she could help Mrs. Weston without breaking her promise to her.

"I wouldn't want to see her upset, Nat. I think she is a wonderful person. We spent a lot of time together today."

Nat smiled. "Yes, I know. It isn't like Mother to get involved with someone so quickly, but she seems to have taken an instant liking to you."

Sharon flushed with pleasure. "I would like us to be friends." She hesitated for a moment before adding, "Do you think she is well, Nat? Sometimes she looks so strained and tired."

There, she thought, I have dropped a hint without breaking my promise to Mrs. Weston.

"I know, Sharon," Nat replied heavily. "She has been looking that way for some weeks now, but when I ask her to see the doctor she only says it is a bit of old age creeping in."

"Can't you just fetch the doctor in? Surely she wouldn't refuse to see him?"

Nat laughed shortly. "Wait until you know her better and you won't ask that. If she decided not to see him, nobody on God's earth would be able to make her. She can be very stubborn."

I have already had a taste of that, Sharon thought, but she couldn't tell Nat that without breaking her promise.

"Anyway," Nat said in a brisker tone, "I had better show you one or two things, then you can get off."

He had a difficult time finding the different things he wanted to show her, not that Sharon was surprised. She wondered how he managed to keep on top of the business side of running the station when everything was in such a mess. As Nat talked about letters needing answering and forms to be filled in etc., Sharon was thinking the first thing she needed to do was get everything filed properly.

They were interrupted by Nell bringing in the coffee. Sharon poured it out, handing one to Nat, but he didn't stop to drink it. He just carried on with what he was doing, so Sharon felt obliged to do the same, sipping at it when she could.

"You can spend each morning working for me," Nat went on to say, "then help my mother in the afternoon. She usually rests after lunch until she has tea, so you can please yourself what you do in that time. Within reason," he added sternly as he caught the glimmer of mischief in her face.

"If you can spend from tea time until you have to get ready for dinner with my mother, she will be more than satisfied," he continued. "The evenings, and weekends of course, are your own time. Is that O.K.?"

"Fine," Sharon agreed. She was really looking forward to it. "It sounds just great."

Nat smiled. "That's about it then. By the way, do you ride?"

Sharon looked surprised. "Not very expertly, I'm afraid. I haven't had all that much chance."

"It is essential out here to be able to ride, that is if you don't want to be tied to the homestead altogether. I think I'll get Mitch to take you out."

"Who's Mitch?" Sharon asked.

"The best ringer we've got," Nat explained. "There is nothing he doesn't know about the stock. He has been with us about twenty years. He rode in one day looking for casual work and never left."

"He must like it here," Sharon commented.

Nat looked at her quickly, suspecting sarcasm, but seemed satisfied by the open smile he received. "That's it then," he said. "You can get off to bed now if you like."

Sharon left the office feeling like a schoolgirl dismissed from the headmaster's presence. Still, she thought, Nat had been reasonably friendly. It was surprising how much better it made her feel. If only there wasn't Miranda, she thought again.

She was feeling ready for bed. The combination of the travelling and excitement had made her very tired. She went through to the lounge, where she hoped to find Mrs. Weston, in order to say goodnight.

She found her alone in the lounge, sitting in the glow from a single standard lamp. Soft music issued from the stereogram in the corner. The curtains had been drawn across the windows and the room was cosy and homely.

"Hello, Mrs. Weston. Sorry to disturb you but I have just come to say goodnight."

Mrs. Weston turned to Sharon with a smile. "Are you very tired, my dear, or will you keep me company for a few minutes?" she asked.

"I'd love to stay," Sharon replied promptly. "This is a lovely room, and you have got my favourite music on too."

"Come and sit down by me, my dear," Mrs. Weston invited, indicating the side of the sofa nearest to her chair. "It's nice to have some female company. That is the worst thing in the Outback, really. We get visitors of course, and we can also have a chat over the radio, but it is not the same. I would have liked a daughter to talk to. I didn't miss it when Josh was alive. I didn't see much of him during the day of course, but we always spent the evenings together."

"What about Nat and Pete?" Sharon asked. "Don't they sit with you at all?"

"Nat does sometimes, when he isn't too busy of course, but with being out on the run all day, it means he has things to do in the office in the evenings."

"Perhaps he will be able to spend more time with

you if I can take most of the office work off his shoulders," Sharon said.

"Perhaps you can both sit with me," Mrs. Weston answered. "Pete prefers to join the ringers for a beer and a game of cards or something."

"He won't be able to do that when he marries Janie," Sharon put it.

"You know about Janie?" Mrs. Weston asked in surprise.

"Nat told me earlier this evening," Sharon replied. She laughed. "He warned me off Pete, but there was no need to. Pete understands I feel nothing but friendship for him."

Mrs. Weston heaved a sigh of relief. "Oh I am glad to hear that. I would have hated to see you break your heart over him, because deep in his heart it will always be Janie with him."

"There is no fear of that," Sharon assured her. She hesitated for a moment. "Will Nat be marrying Miranda soon?" she asked casually, looking down at her hands.

She failed to see the speculative gleam which came into Mrs. Weston's eyes before she answered. "For someone who only met my family a few days ago, you seem remarkably well informed."

Sharon raised her head, flushing slightly. "I'm sorry, I didn't mean to sound inquisitive."

"Don't be sorry, my dear," Mrs. Weston told her. "You can ask what you like. Now, about Nat. I don't think he will marry Miranda. If he had wanted to, he would have done so years ago. Nat will only marry for love, like his father, and I am certain he doesn't love Miranda. I know Miranda would have married him a long time ago, and it would have been a suitable match, because she was born and bred on a cattle station too, and knows her way around. Love is more important than that though, isn't it?"

"Oh yes," Sharon agreed. "Any girl who loved her husband would change her way of life in order to be with him and help him all she could. I know I would, without the slightest hesitation."

Sharon was afraid she had said too much, but Mrs. Weston didn't appear to have noticed anything. "I did that, and Josh and I were terribly happy until the day he died."

"I can see that," Sharon murmured, envious of this charming woman's memories.

Mrs. Weston pulled herself together. "Would you like some hot chocolate or a cup of tea before we go up?" she asked.

"I would enjoy a cup of tea," Sharon admitted.

Mrs. Weston rose to her feet. "I'll go and make some. The lubras have already gone home."

"If you tell me where everything is, I will do it," Sharon offered.

"We'll go together. If you watch where everything is, you can make it next time."

The kitchen was large and full of every modern gadget. Everywhere was sparkling clean, with no clutter anywhere.

Sharon watched carefully as Mrs. Weston set the kettle going, then out of various cupboards fetched the tea-caddy, teapot and sugar. She took the milk out of the fridge and set it beside two cups and saucers which had been on the dresser.

"We won't bother taking a tray through, if you don't mind," Mrs. Weston said.

The kettle boiled quickly and she made the tea. "It was so different when I was first married," she told

Sharon. "We didn't have electricity in those days, and everything was done on an old range."

"That must have caused problems," Sharon said. "That reminds me, I never saw any power lines as we came in."

"That is because there aren't any," Nat's voice came from the doorway. "Is there enough tea for me, Mother?" he added.

"Of course," Mrs. Weston replied, going to fetch another cup and saucer.

"We have got our own generators," Nat explained to Sharon. "We have a main one and a back up, in case the main one breaks down."

"Help yourself to sugar," Mrs. Weston interrupted. "Shall we take it through to the lounge?"

"O.K." Nat replied, taking two cups and saucers. "Can you bring the other one Sharon?"

"Yes, of course," she replied.

They settled down in the lounge. Nat began telling his mother about some poddy-dodgers he had been warned about.

Sharon nearly choked on her tea. "Whatever are poddy-dodgers?" she laughed when she could speak again.

Nat grinned. "I forgot you are a newcomer. Poddy-dodgers are men who steal the unbranded calves. It is a lucrative, if dangerous, business. We aren't usually bothered with too much of it, but there seems to be a spate of it at the moment."

"They have to be highly organized," Mrs. Weston said. "Just think of the distances involved."

"They know what they are doing, right enough," Nat answered grimly. "We'll have to alert the stock-men."

Sharon was having difficulty keeping her eyes open and she stifled a yawn.

"Get off to bed, Sharon," Nat said kindly. "You look tuckered out."

"I must admit I do feel rather tired," she agreed. "I'll just take these cups into the kitchen and rinse them, then I'll be off."

"Never mind that," Nat told her firmly. "I'll see to those. If you don't get to bed I won't get any work out of you tomorrow."

Sharon looked up sharply, but Nat was openly smiling, so she smiled back. "I'll go up then," she said. "Goodnight Mrs. Weston, goodnight Nat."

They chorused goodnight, Mrs. Weston adding, "I will be up myself very soon."

It was as much as Sharon could do to crawl into the bathroom to clean her teeth and have a quick wash. She felt really worn out, and as soon as her head touched the pillow she was asleep, hearing nothing until she was woken up in the morning by Nell bringing her a cup of tea.

Ten

Sharon was surprised to find Mrs. Weston already in the kitchen when she went in to return her cup.

"Good morning, Mrs. Weston," she said brightly.

"Good morning, Sharon," Mrs. Weston replied with a smile. She caught sight of the cup in Sharon's hand. "You needn't have brought that down, my dear," she told her. "Nell would have fetched it later."

"That's all right," Sharon replied. "I didn't expect tea in bed anyway."

"Well I thought all the English liked one," Mrs. Weston said. "I have arranged for you to have one each morning."

"That is very kind of you," Sharon replied, pleased with Mrs. Weston's thoughtfulness.

"What would you like for breakfast?" Mrs. Weston asked, ignoring Sharon's thanks.

"Just toast please, then I'll make a start in the office." Sharon grimaced. "I haven't made up my mind where to begin really. There are papers everywhere."

"I am sure you will cope admirably," Mrs. Weston said.

She turned to the elder of the Aborigine girls present. "See to Miss Maine's toast and make a pot of coffee, Minnie."

The smiling Minnie hurried to do as she was bid. "I will see you later, Sharon," Mrs. Weston continued. "I am going down to see the child of one of our Aborigine stockmen. Her mother said she wasn't well and I must check to see if we need the doctor."

It was obvious the Westons looked after their workers, Sharon thought as she munched her toast. Mrs. Weston had shown her concern over the child's welfare. It seemed as if it was one big happy family.

She finished her breakfast, then headed for the office. It was going to be a big job getting everything sorted out, she thought. She decided to rearrange the filing cabinet and re-label it first, then she would have somewhere to put everything she picked up from around the room.

She guessed that any letter which had been written on had already been attended to, so she put those in the bottom drawer, leaving everything which was unmarked for Nat to go through. Agricultural literature went in another drawer, and papers which were obviously accounts she put in another.

Just before ten o'clock, Nat came in carrying a tray loaded with coffee and biscuits. "I can see I won't know the place soon," he remarked, noticing the progress Sharon had already made.

Sharon, caught unawares, couldn't control the look of welcome in her face as she turned from the filing cabinet. Nat looked at her oddly, but only said, "Nell was about to bring this in, so I begged a cup too."

Sharon pulled herself together, mentally kicking herself for nearly letting her secret out. "I didn't expect to see you this morning," she said.

Sharon noticed Nat's jeans and check shirt were streaked with dirt, and wondered what he had been doing.

"I have been out on the run since seven," he told her. "I wouldn't be in now except Mother sent a message that one of the kids is ill, and she wants the doctor. She suspects appendicitis," he added with a frown.

"Oh, poor thing," Sharon said. "How old is he?"

"It's a girl, and she is only nine," Nat replied.

A voice suddenly issuing from the radio receiver made Sharon jump.

"Here we go," Nat said. "There is a Flying Doctor session at ten each morning," he explained. "Anyone can talk to the Doc, and he will advise on treatment, or arrange a call if he thinks it is necessary. We have to do a lot of doctoring ourselves, being so far away from each other, and we carry an extensive First Aid and drug kit."

Sharon listened, fascinated, to the different voices giving their call sign and explaining symptoms, and the doctor giving his opinion. He seemed to know everyone, asking about old patients as well as present ones. Then it was Nat's turn. He gave the Weston Downs call sign and identified himself.

"Hiya, Nat," the doctor's voice came over. "What can I do for you?"

"Hi, Doc. We've got an Abo kid, suspected appendicitis."

"What are the symptoms?" the doctor asked sharply.

"Pains and tenderness in her side, and vomiting," Nat told him.

"You could be right," the doctor replied. "There again, it could be a form of food poisoning. You know what kids are for eating strange things."

"Yes sure," Nat said with a laugh.

"Anyway, Nat, I had better fly in and take a look at her. I'll be with you in a couple of hours."

"Thanks, Doc," Nat said, then turned to Sharon. "It is better to be safe than sorry, isn't it?"

"Of course," Sharon agreed. "I was just thinking, there isn't much privacy about ailments, is there? Everybody knows when you have spoken to the doctor."

"True," Nat answered. "Everybody understands though, and there is one advantage in that if anyone is taken ill and everybody knows about it, help floods in. I have known a neighbour drive over five hundred miles to take over the running of a homestead."

Sharon was impressed. "The rewards of modern science are remarkable."

"Sure are," Nat agreed. "Can you imagine what it used to be like years ago, before radio and the Flying Doctor services? If anyone was taken ill, they had to be taken sometimes hundreds of miles over uninhabited and hostile territory to the nearest township for treatment."

"It doesn't bear thinking about," Sharon said

with a shudder. "The death rate must have been pretty high."

"I don't know really," Nat replied. "I think folks were tougher in those days. They had to be, to survive."

Nat was a natural born survivor, Sharon thought. He would probably have enjoyed the hardships of the past, seeing them as a challenge. His determination and strength of character would have helped him to succeed where others failed.

"Has the Flying Doctor finished now?" she asked, noticing the radio was silent.

"Yes, until tomorrow. The School of the Air will be on soon, so I'll turn the receiver off, then you won't be bothered by it. I tell you what though, get Mother to bring you to listen to the chat session. At six o'clock each evening the women take over the airways for an hour. They can catch up on all the gossip then," he added with a grin.

"Men are usually worse gossips than women," Sharon told him indignantly.

"No way," Nat laughed. "Men only say what they have got to say. Women say whatever everybody else has been saying."

Deciding not to get involved in a battle of words with Nat, Sharon stood up. "Well, I've got work to do," she said pointedly.

Nat grinned. "And I'm in the way, right? I can take the hint."

With that, he had gone, leaving Sharon to her thoughts and her cleaning-up operations. Some time later, the drone of a plane's engine sent her out on to the veranda, shading her eyes with her hand. At last she spotted the plane circling overhead, getting ready to land.

The utility truck screeched to a halt in front of her. "Want to come?" Nat asked from behind the wheel.

Sharon didn't hesitate. "Yes please," she replied eagerly. Nat leaned over to open the door for her and reached out a hand to help her in. She grasped it and hauled herself up, glad she was wearing slacks because the step was quite high. Nat seemed to hold onto her hand longer than really necessary, and her heart began to pound.

It was over in a few seconds but she could still feel the pressure of Nat's hand a long time after he let her go to put the truck into motion. They arrived at the airstrip just as the plane landed. Sharon followed Nat when he walked towards the plane. The door opened and steps were let down, then a man and a woman stepped down.

"Hi, Doc," Nat said, shaking the man's hand.

"Hi, Nat," the doctor replied. "How are you doing?"

"Just fine thanks," Nat answered.

"You don't know my nurse, do you? This is Lorna Brent."

"Hi there, Nurse," Nat said, adding, "Say, aren't you the one who came to be a private nurse at Parker Ridge?"

The pretty dark-haired nurse laughed. "That's right. No secrets can be kept around here."

Sharon saw her look sideways at the doctor, immediately giving her secret away. She was in love with him. That is why she stayed on, Sharon thought. I hope she has better luck than me.

"Sharon," Nat's voice recalled her. "This is our Flying Doctor, Steve Carey, and Nurse Lorna Brent. This is Sharon Maine, my new office help."

Sharon took Steve's outstretched hand, taking an

instant liking to the good-looking young doctor, then smiled at Nurse Brent.

"How do you do?" she said.

"That accent has got to be English," Steve said with a smile. "You're a long way from home."

Home is where the heart is, Sharon thought, right here, but aloud only said, "Just seeing a bit of the world."

"Don't blame you," Steve answered before turning to Nat. "Right. Where's my patient?"

"It will be a tight squeeze," Nat remarked as he got behind the wheel of the truck.

"Don't worry about me. I'll ride in the back," Steve said. "Lorna can ride up front with you."

He put his bag into the back of the truck and climbed in after it, sitting on the side. Of necessity, Sharon had to slide over the seat to allow the nurse to get in. Nat's closeness did strange things to her senses so she concentrated on talking to the nurse.

The ride was more comfortable than when Pete had driven her when she first arrived, so she wasn't thrown against Nat, much to her relief. The truck skirted several buildings before coming to a halt in front of a small cabin. They all got out of the truck as Mrs. Weston appeared in the doorway, her relief at seeing them very apparent.

"I'm glad you have arrived," she told Steve. "The poor little girl is much worse. I think she is feverish."

She led the way in, followed by the doctor and nurse and Nat. Sharon was left standing by the door feeling very out of place. She looked through the door, feeling her eyes prick at the sight of the little black girl lying on a camp bed, whilst Steve examined her with gentle fingers, talking to her quietly all the time.

The little girl's eyes were bright with fever and she was crying quietly, while her mother looked on, wringing her hands in distress.

A few moments later, they all came out again, and Sharon looked anxiously at Steve. She feared the worst when she saw his grave unsmiling face. He ran his hand through his hair.

"It's appendicitis, all right, Nat, and a bad one too. Why must these people leave everything to the last minute? It is ready to burst and I haven't got time to get her back to the base hospital. I'll have to operate here."

"Here?" Sharon cried involuntarily. "You can't operate in there."

"He means at our own hospital," Nat said sharply, then relented as he saw her stricken face. He put his hand on her shoulder. "I forgot you don't know your way around yet. Our hospital, and I use the term loosely, is that building over there. It is only a couple of beds and a surgery really, but it serves our needs for most things."

"I'm sorry, Nat," Sharon apologized, near to tears. "I shouldn't have said anything."

"Don't worry," Nat told her before turning to Steve. "Right, we'd better get organized. What do you want doing, Steve?"

"The table needs scrubbing and the sterilizer will have to be switched on. I will need the rest of my equipment from the plane, including the portable anaesthetic machine."

"I'll fetch those," Nat offered.

"Go with him Lorna, to help: Don't forget the gowns."

"O.K., Steve," Lorna replied quietly. Sharon

couldn't understand how she could take it all so calmly.

"Mrs. Weston," Steve continued, "if you and Sharon come with me, we'll get the hospital ready."

Sharon was glad to be doing something. She saw that Mrs. Weston was looking a bit grey, and begged her to go back to the house.

"When I have done all I can," Mrs. Weston replied firmly.

Sharon was surprised when she saw the hospital. The single-storey building housed modern equipment, and everything was clean and shiny.

Mrs. Weston filled the sterilizer and switched it on whilst the doctor checked the drugs cabinet, then Mrs. Weston went up to the house to fetch linen to make a bed up.

Under the doctor's instructions, Sharon scrubbed the table, then fetched a trolley for the instruments. By the time she had finished, Nat and Lorna were back with the equipment from the plane.

Lorna put the instruments in the sterilizer which was now bubbling merrily, whilst Nat set the anaesthetic unit by the top of the table, then the doctor checked it, making sure everything was just right.

At last everything was ready except for Steve and Lorna scrubbing up, so he signalled Nat to fetch the little girl.

"I'll have the instruments on the trolley," Steve told Lorna, "then you can see to the anaesthetic."

Nat and an Aborigine carried the little girl in and placed her carefully on the prepared table.

"Sharon, see what you can do with her mother, will you," Nat asked. "She is almost hysterical."

Sharon hurried off to the woman, who was sitting on the floor outside, weeping uncontrollably. She knelt down beside her, putting a comforting arm around her shoulders.

"She will be all right," she assured her soothingly. "The doctor and nurse know what they are doing, and she'll be better in next to no time."

Sharon mentally crossed her fingers, praying that she was right. She knew that if the appendix burst, it would be touch and go, especially under these conditions.

"What is your little girl's name?" she continued. The woman broke off to say, "Emily," then carried on as before.

Sharon continued talking calmly, telling her that she had had the same operation when she was a little girl, and had got over it quickly. She heaved a sigh of relief when the woman began to calm down until only short sniffs and sobs showed her distress.

Sharon was suddenly aware that they weren't alone, and she looked up quickly to see Nat standing behind her. She was surprised to see a look of compassion, or was it tenderness, on his face, but this quickly disappeared, leaving her to wonder if she had imagined it.

She stood up and went over to him. "What's happening?" she whispered, mindful of the woman sitting a few feet away, rocking back and forth.

"They have started," Nat answered in a low voice. "If all goes well it won't be long."

They stood silently together, their thoughts with the little girl whose life was in danger. "Her name is Emily," Sharon suddenly said.

"I know," Nat replied quietly, putting a comforting arm round her. "She will be all right," he continued.

"Steve is a brilliant doctor. He could have made the big time in any city, but he has chosen to devote his life to the Outback."

Sharon was content to stand in the shelter of Nat's arm. There was nothing sexual in the contact, but she was conscious of the warmth and reassurance flowing from him.

How long they stood there she didn't know, but suddenly the waiting was over. They both turned as they heard a movement in the doorway, their expressions anxious. Steve stood there, pulling his mask down. He looked drawn but pleased.

"It's all over," he said quietly. "She is going to be all right."

Sharon suddenly felt weak at the knees. "Oh, thank God," she said, her eyes filling with tears of relief.

"Will you help me get her into bed, Nat?" Steve asked, then turned to Sharon. "You can tell the mother she can come in and sit by her in about five minutes time."

Sharon nodded and went over to the woman, who hadn't moved and seemed oblivious to everything except her inner anxiety. She knelt down by her and touched her gently on the shoulder. The woman jerked her head up, her eyes filled with fear.

Sharon smiled. "It is all over. Emily is going to be all right."

It didn't seem to sink in for a minute, so Sharon repeated, "Emily is all right."

The radiance which suddenly filled the woman's face was something Sharon would never forget. The woman began to thank her over and over again, which embarrassed her enormously. She hadn't done anything.

"You must thank the doctor, not me," Sharon explained. "He said you can go and sit with Emily now, but she will be asleep for some time yet."

The woman didn't care about that. She scrambled to her feet, then looked to Sharon for guidance. Sharon took her arm and led her to the door. Nat was just coming out.

"Can she go in now?" Sharon asked him, then took the woman inside when Nat nodded. They went through the room where Steve had operated. Lorna was busy clearing up and she smiled encouragement as they passed.

Steve was standing by the bed, taking the little girl's pulse. He smiled at them, putting her arm down and fetching a chair for the mother to use.

"She is all right," he told her with a smile, indicating she should sit down.

The woman immediately began her thanks again, but Steve interrupted her. "You can stop a few minutes now, then come back later. Your little girl is very tired and needs to rest. Do you understand?"

The woman nodded, then forgot Steve and Sharon as she concentrated on the still figure lying in bed.

"I'm afraid we'll have a job to move her," Steve said ruefully as he and Sharon walked away. "Our only hope is that her husband will control her."

"Where is he, by the way?" Sharon asked. "You would have thought he would have been here."

"Nat said he has sent for him, but he will be a while yet because he is working in the far pastures."

Sharon was pleased to hear it. It was clear the woman needed someone's support for the next few days, and hoped Nat would keep her husband close to the homestead.

She joined Nat and Mrs. Weston outside, Steve excusing himself whilst he helped Lorna finish off. She was worried about how strained Mrs. Weston was looking, but could say nothing in front of Nat.

The talk of course was about Emily, and how fortunate she had been, then Mrs. Weston said she would go to see about some coffee, then hurry up the lunch. In the excitement, nobody had given a thought to eating.

She seemed in a hurry to go, and it suddenly struck Sharon why. She didn't want the doctor to look too closely at her in case he suspected something. She bit her lip, wishing she hadn't promised not to say anything. It would have been ideal for Steve to have a look at her whilst he was already on the station. Mrs. Weston had only just left when Steve and Lorna appeared.

"I'll leave her an hour until I'm sure her condition is stable, then we will get her into the plane and take her to the base hospital," Steve told them. "She'll need to be watched closely for a few days, at least until the tubes are out."

"Will her mother go too?" Sharon asked.

"No way," Steve answered emphatically. "We'll have a problem persuading her to let the child go. I hope her husband comes soon."

"He should be here before you are ready to leave," Nat assured him. "Now then, are you coming for some lunch?"

"Would it be too much trouble if we have ours here?" Steve asked. "We can't really leave our patient."

"I'm sorry, Steve, I didn't think," Nat replied. "I'll send it down to you then, see you a bit later."

Sharon glanced back as she and Nat walked off, in

time to see Steve and Lorna going back inside, their arms around each other. So she had been right about Lorna. Lucky Lorna, it looked as if Steve felt the same way.

"I will forgo my free time today," she told Nat as they neared the house. "I have lost a lot of time."

"You most certainly will not," Nat told her. "I asked you to come, so I will take the blame. Anyway, I have arranged with Mitch for him to give you a refresher course in riding, starting this afternoon. Meet him in the stockyards and he'll fix you up with a quiet mount."

"Hadn't you better cancel it, with this trouble?" Sharon asked.

"No need," Nat replied. "Steve will be taking Emily to the hospital soon, and everything will be back to normal."

I do hope so, Sharon thought, her mind on Mrs. Weston's strained face.

Eleven

Sharon's hands felt clammy as she reached the stockyard. She wasn't looking forward to her first meeting with a horse for a long time. She had had lessons when she was at school, but had never been very good at it.

She had eaten lunch with Mrs. Weston and Nat, then Pete had come in off the run. He had heard of the excitement, but didn't seem particularly concerned about dear little Emily, much to Sharon's disgust. He didn't have the same attitude as Nat, who really cared about people. The unknown Janie would need to be strong-willed to settle him to any responsibility.

Pete had offered to take Sharon riding himself, but Nat had reminded him there was other work for him to do. Pete had sulked for a while before his natural good humour was restored.

Sharon had accompanied Nat to see little Emily off. She had been carefully carried out to the plane without disturbance, which pleased Steve. He and Lorna climbed into the plane after assuring them that he would send regular bulletins over the air.

Sharon was surprised at the difference in Emily's mother when her husband was there. She was perfectly calm and controlled, and let Emily go without any fuss, although her face registered her anxiety.

After the plane had taken off, Nat told Sharon where to find the stockyards, saying he would be down later to see how things were going. Sharon hoped desperately that he wouldn't, because she knew his presence would unnerve her, at least until she had gained some confidence.

A middle-aged man with a dark wrinkled face and piercing blue eyes came to meet her. He smiled and touched his big slouch hat. "Hi there, ma'am," he drawled. "I'm Mitch. The boss said I was to give you a few pointers on riding."

"Yes, that's right," Sharon said, beaming back at him. She knew right away that she was going to get on with him. "I am afraid I haven't ridden for a long time, so I hope you have got a nice quiet horse for me."

"Don't you fret, ma'am," Mitch said. "The boss said I was to take real good care of you."

Sharon flushed with pleasure. Fancy Nat saying that, she thought happily.

"Come and get acquainted with Daisy," Mitch continued. "One of the best stock horses I've ever come across, but she is a bit old now, so she stays at home to enjoy her retirement."

He took Sharon into the home paddock where a big brown animal stood contentedly, watching their approach with interest. She whinnied as they reached her, and nuzzled Mitch's outstretched hand.

"You are a greedy lady," Mitch told her, affectionately rubbing her nose before reaching into his shirt pocket for a lump of sugar.

Sharon laughed. "It looks as if she knows what to expect when she sees you," she said.

"Ought to by now," Mitch replied. "I worked her a long time before she retired. Here, you give her the sugar and let her get to know you. Keep talking to her all the time, and she loves to have her nose rubbed."

Sharon held the sugar out gingerly, hoping she wouldn't lose her hand. Daisy took it delicately, hardly touching Sharon's hand. Sharon then felt more confident as she reached up to rub her nose.

"There's a good girl, Daisy," she said softly. "We are going to be great friends, aren't we?"

In answer, Daisy nuzzled her nose into Sharon's shoulder, blowing gently down her neck.

"She's your friend all right, ma'am," Mitch told her in his slow drawl. "Never seen her take to anyone so quickly before."

"Oh, do you really think so?" Sharon said delightedly, "and please call me Sharon."

Mitch smiled. "Thank you, ma'am, I mean Sharon. Now if you're ready, we'll get you mounted."

Funnily enough, Sharon didn't feel nervous when she sat in the saddle. Mitch adjusted the stirrups and tightened the girth. He then walked round the paddock holding Daisy's bridle, giving Sharon a chance to get the feel of the horse underneath her.

"O.K. Sharon, now you go alone. Just a gentle walk first. Don't worry, I'll be right beside you."

Sharon took up the slack on the reins, and squeezed her knees against the horse. Daisy immediately broke quickly, nearly unseating Sharon. She was glad Mitch was there to grab the bridle.

"Thank you, Mitch," she said shakily. "I don't know what happened."

"You squeezed too hard," Mitch explained. "Remember, Daisy might be retired, but deep inside she is still a stock horse, trained to respond to the slightest command. Now try again, and this time not so hard."

Sharon held her breath, and squeezed very gently. This time she got it right, and Daisy walked on sedately. Mitch made her walk round the paddock several times, stopping and starting again until he felt she was all right.

"Now try putting her into a trot," he ordered.

Daisy obediently upped her pace at Sharon's command, and Sharon went immediately into a rising trot. Mitch stopped her straight away.

"What was wrong?" Sharon asked in a puzzled voice.

"Riding that way may be all right for a pleasant few minutes in an English park, but not here, where you may have to spend hours at a time in the saddle. Besides, Daisy didn't like it. Her ears were twitching."

Sharon turned astonished eyes to Daisy's ears. "Can you really tell what she's thinking by looking at her ears?"

Mitch laughed. "Sure. If they are upright and

alert, she is enjoying herself. If they are twitching, she isn't very happy about something. And if they ever go down flat, you can look out. It means she is real mad and likely to do anything."

Sharon eyed Daisy's ears with new respect. "Remind me to jump then if ever they are flat," she told Mitch, earning herself a smile of appreciation.

She tried the trot several times, feeling as if she was getting every bone in her body jolted, then at last, when she was least expecting it, she suddenly found herself moving with the horse.

Mitch signified approval, then told her to go into a canter. This proved no problem at all, and when Mitch told her that was enough she rode over to him with her face alight with pleasure.

"You've done real fine," Mitch congratulated her. "Tomorrow we'll ride out together and see how you get on."

"Thank you very much, Mitch," Sharon said with a smile. "It was all due to you. I have done better in a couple of hours than I did during all the riding lessons I had at school."

Mitch looked slightly uncomfortable at the praise. "Don't forget Daisy. She behaved real well."

Sharon leaned forward to fondle Daisy's ears. "Thank you too, Daisy. You are a lovely lady."

Daisy tossed her head to signify she agreed with that, then Sharon dismounted.

"I'll see to Daisy today," Mitch said, "but from tomorrow you will have to rub her down, and also saddle her yourself."

Sharon didn't mind that, and told him so, then looked up at the sound of approaching hoofbeats. It was Nat, astride a big black stallion. She didn't try to conceal a smile of welcome she gave him.

"You're looking mighty pleased with yourself," he told her.

"She's done real well, Boss," Mitch told him. "I'll take her out tomorrow if that's all right with you."

"Good man," Nat approved. "At this rate we'll soon have her out on the run."

Sharon flushed with pleasure, telling Nat it was all due to Mitch and Daisy. Mitch chuckled. "So she thinks," he murmured. He took Daisy's bridle and led her off, leaving Sharon staring up at Nat, thinking how well he sat his horse. The stallion began snorting and pawing the ground, hating the inactivity, but Nat held him easily.

"I came to tell you that Mother is waiting for you to have tea with her. She's in her sitting-room. I'll see you before dinner," Nat said. He touched the stallion's flanks and the horse leapt forward. Sharon watched as they galloped away, man and beast joined together as one. Suddenly she remembered the dream where she was being chased by a dark man on a big horse. She shivered, realizing it could have been Nat.

A few minutes later, Sharon knocked on Mrs. Weston's door, and entered at her bidding. Mrs. Weston sat in the chair, the tea tray already on the table in front of her.

"I saw you coming," Mrs. Weston said. "I knew by the time the tea arrived you would have had time to freshen up after your riding. How did you get on? Do sit down, my dear."

Sharon sat down, taking the cup off Mrs. Weston. "I am feeling very pleased with myself," she answered. "I didn't fall off once."

"I'm glad to hear it. Are you glad Nat suggested it now?"

"Oh yes," Sharon told her. "Mitch is taking me out for a proper ride tomorrow. I'm really looking forward to it."

"That will be nice for you," Mrs. Weston smiled. "I hope you will still find time to help me."

Sharon looked shocked. "Of course I will," she replied. "Even if it wasn't part of my job, I would still want to do it."

"Thank you, my dear." Mrs. Weston patted Sharon's hand. "When we've finished tea we'll make a start. There is a big box of letters and records in that cupboard over there that we must put into order first."

Mrs. Weston's voice sounded weak, and Sharon looked at her closely. Her afternoon rest hadn't helped her much, for she still looked white and strained.

"Are you sure you feel up to it?" she asked quietly. "You look a little tired."

"I am positive my dear," Mrs. Weston replied firmly. "It is only because I didn't sleep much this afternoon. I was thinking of poor little Emily, poorly and away from her mother and father."

"You mustn't worry about her," Sharon said. "Children are very resilient. She'll soon be thinking it is a big adventure, then she'll come bouncing back home feeling full of herself."

"I do hope you are right. Anyway, we are sure to get a message this evening, then we can put her parents' minds at rest too. They must be very upset."

They finished their tea and set to work. Sharon was concerned with the way Mrs. Weston looked, and was glad when they stopped to get changed for dinner. Perhaps when Nat saw how ill she looked he would insist on contacting the doctor.

She was doomed to disappointment though, for when Mrs. Weston appeared for dinner she had skillfully made up her face to make it appear natural, and she acted as if she was perfectly all right. Only Sharon noticed the strain in her eyes, the sudden darkening as if she was getting spasms of pain.

Sharon excused herself immediately after dinner, saying she needed to rest her aching limbs. Her plan worked. Mrs. Weston said she would leave the men to themselves and have an early night herself. Sharon had known Mrs. Weston wouldn't move first in case Nat or Pete became suspicious, and had deliberately given her the opportunity to go to bed early without anyone else knowing she was feeling poorly.

"Are you sure you are going to be all right?" Sharon asked as they went upstairs together. "Would you like me to sit with you for a while?"

"You are a good girl," Mrs. Weston smiled. "I will go straight to bed and I'll be all right by tomorrow. Thank you anyway."

She was breathless by the time they reached the top and had to stand for a few moments to gather her strength again. Sharon didn't know what to do. She had no right to force Mrs. Weston into anything, but she wished with all her heart she hadn't promised her she wouldn't tell Nat.

She decided to read for a while. She had found a thriller in the bookcase in the office which she thought she would enjoy. She showered and put on a blue nylon nightdress and négligé, then lay on top of the bed, intending to read for a couple of hours.

She felt a bit stiff and sore from the riding, but guessed it would be even worse in the morning when she had stiffened up. Half an hour later, there was a tap on the door and she heard Mrs. Weston calling her. She flung her book down and raced to open the door. She was frightened by the sight which met her.

Mrs. Weston looked really ill. Her lips looked blue against her white face, and her eyes seemed to have sunk in. She stood in her underslip, clutching a hand to her breast.

"My God," Sharon said. "Whatever is the matter?"

"I've got a terrible pain in my chest, and my arm hurts," Mrs. Weston replied faintly. "I feel so ill and I'm frightened. I think I'm going to die."

Sharon put her arm round her and helped her to lie on the bed, covering her with just the bedspread. "I'm sorry Mrs. Weston, I'm going to fetch Nat. I must break my promise not to tell him. I won't allow you to suffer like this."

"All right my dear," Mrs. Weston agreed weakly. When Sharon reached the door, she called her back.

"Make me another promise, Sharon," she pleaded weakly, her eyes misty.

Sharon went down on her knees beside the bed, taking Mrs. Weston's hand in here. "Anything. What is it?"

"If anything happens to me, you'll look after Nat. You love him, don't you?"

Sharon only hesitated a moment. "Yes, with all my heart," she admitted quietly.

"Marry him, child," Mrs. Weston continued. "He loves you too, I think. I have seen the way he watches you. Don't let Miranda come between you. She is wrong . . ."

She broke off as a fiercer pain tore through her chest, then suddenly closed her eyes. Sharon choked back a sob, then raced out onto the landing.

"Nat, Nat, come quickly," she cried, tears running unheeded down her cheeks.

Nat came running out of the lounge, Pete close on his heels. Seeing Sharon's anguish, Nat put his arms round her. "My God, what is it?" he asked urgently.

"It's your mother, Nat. In my room," Sharon sobbed almost incoherently.

Nat's face went white. "Come on, show me."

They raced into Sharon's room where Mrs. Weston lay, just as Sharon had left her. Nat dropped onto his knees by the bed, whilst Pete stood by the door, unwilling or unable to go further in.

"What happened?" Nat asked curtly, taking his mother's pulse. "The pulse is very faint."

Sharon nearly collapsed. She had thought Mrs. Weston was dead.

"What happened?" Nat repeated.

"I think she has had a h—heart attack," Sharon finally stammered.

"Pete, go and put an emergency call through to Steve," Nat ordered.

Pete just stood there, not seeming to understand. Nat muttered something, got to his feet. "Stay with her Sharon. I'll do it myself."

Sharon took Nat's place by the bed. "Pete, why don't you go and see if you can help Nat," she suggested quietly.

Pete didn't hear her. "I must get a call through to Janie," was all he said, then turned and went away.

Sharon thought no more about him. She held onto Mrs. Weston's hand tightly. "Please wake up," she sobbed. "I won't let you die. Nat needs you and

Pete needs you and I need you. What about all those grandchildren?"

Sharon's words seemed to penetrate, for Mrs. Weston opened her eyes again, just as Nat came back in to kneel by Sharon. "I'm all right," she whispered. "It is nice to see you two together. Why don't you kiss her, Nat?"

Sharon blushed and raised her face to Nat's. Please humour her, her eyes begged. Nat's eyes darkened in response, and he lowered his head. Sharon's mind, numbed with anxiety, failed to tell her to curb her response, so as soon as Nat's lips touched hers she was lost. Her lips parted involuntarily, and what was intended to be a light kiss deepened, drawing Sharon's heart out.

When they eventually parted, they looked guiltily at Mrs. Weston, but she was smiling, tears running down her cheeks. "I loved my Josh like that," she whispered, then closed her eyes again.

Nat immediately felt for her pulse, then breathed deeply. "Still the same, thank goodness," he said.

"Nat, I . . ." Sharon began.

Nat put a finger against her lips. "We'll talk later, honey. I've got a lot to do. Steve is flying in straight away and I must set up flares on the airstrip for him to land by. Thank God his plane is a new one, equipped for night flying, or I don't know what we would have done. Where's Pete?" he added curtly. "Why isn't he here when I need him?"

"I don't know," Sharon replied. "He muttered something about calling Janie, then disappeared. Don't be too hard on him Nat, please. He has had a shock, and he isn't as strong-willed as you."

Nat frowned for a moment, then nodded. "You're

right, honey. At least he had the sense to think of Janie. Perhaps this will make him grow up at last."

"It will please your mother," Sharon said quietly, her eyes going to the still figure.

"You won't leave her, will you?" Nat asked as he got up to leave. "I don't want her left alone."

"Trust me, Nat," she begged.

"I do," Nat replied quietly, a strange light in his eyes.

All through her lonely vigil, Sharon's thoughts ran riot. Even through her anxiety for Mrs. Weston, a faint hope was rising in her heart. Could Mrs. Weston have been right? Did Nat love her too? She forced herself to be calm and damp down her emotions. She couldn't bear it if she had her hopes and dreams dashed.

Tears filled her eyes as she knelt by Mrs. Weston, not caring about the cramp she was feeling. She closed her eyes and prayed to God, first for the safe recovery of the woman she had begun to love as a second mother in so short a time, and second for the fulfilment of her own dreams.

The drone of a plane engine alerted her, and she raised her head. She had no idea how long she had been there, only that Mrs. Weston had hung onto a thread of life, and the doctor had at last arrived. She heaved a sigh of relief. Now at least something could be done. She had felt so inadequate, only able to comfort a woman who wasn't even aware of her presence.

The sound of running feet on the stairs brought her to her feet. Nat strode in with Steve and Lorna close behind.

"Any change?" he asked quietly.

Sharon shook her head, standing back to allow

Steve and Lorna to get to the bed. Steve examined Mrs. Weston thoroughly. At last he stood up, his face grave.

"You were right," he said quietly. "It was a heart attack. I must get her to the base hospital immediately. I don't carry the specialized equipment I need. I'll give her an injection now to keep her as stable as possible, then get off right away."

Nat nodded. "I'm coming too if you don't mind," he said to Steve. "Pete must take over here. I intend staying with Mother."

"Fair enough," Steve agreed. "Let's get started."

They had brought a stretcher from the plane in case it was needed, and this was fetched upstairs. Mrs. Weston was put gently onto it, covered up and strapped in. Pete had appeared, now looking absolutely calm, and it was he who helped Nat carry the stretcher.

Sharon accompanied them out onto the veranda, bending down to kiss Mrs. Weston's cheek gently before the stretcher was laid in the back of the truck, with Nat, Steve and Lorna cushioning it. Pete got in behind the wheel and the truck crawled away.

News of the unhappy event had spread like wildfire, and it seemed as if the entire population of the station had turned up to see Mrs. Weston taken away. Everyone, white and Aborigine alike, stood around in small groups, some murmuring quietly, but most silent.

Between the outbuildings Sharon could see the brightness of the flares set out on the airstrip, throwing strange shadows into the surrounding area. The sound of the truck carried clearly on the still silent night air, and the moon looked silently on.

Nat would probably stop to give Pete a few last-minute instructions before following his mother onto the plane, Sharon thought, when the truck had stopped.

At last the plane took off, its fuselage reflecting the flickering light of the flares. Sharon's heart winged its message after Nat. "God Bless, take care, I love you."

Twelve

Sharon awoke feeling rather groggy. Her head ached and her eyes burned. She had had a bad night, tossing and turning for a long time, her thoughts with Nat and Mrs. Weston. When she had eventually dropped off to sleep she again had the dream of being chased by a dark horseman, and then lying in a man's arms under a tree. The difference this time was that the man was clearly Nat.

She and Pete had talked for a while after he returned from seeing the plane off. She made some tea and they drank it sitting in the kitchen.

Pete had suddenly become a different person. First the shock of his mother's serious illness, then being given the responsibility of running the station during Nat's absence had combined to bring the serious side of his nature to the forefront.

He had contacted Janie to ask her if she could come to stay at Weston Downs for a while, and she had said she would arrive sometime the next day, all being well.

"You have made up your mind about her then?" Sharon asked.

Pete looked a little shamefaced. "I suddenly feel ready to get married and settle down on Waringa Station. We have owned it for years, and Nat always said it would be mine when I married."

Sharon was genuinely pleased for him, and told him so, adding, "I don't know why you have left it so long."

"Nor me, now," he replied. "I only wanted to enjoy myself. Life is so short, and marriage is for ever."

"That explains me and all the other girls," Sharon told him mischievously.

Pete was embarrassed. "Look, Sharon, I'm sorry about that. I really did, and still do, like you a lot."

"Don't worry about that. I understand," she assured him. "Just be happy with Janie, that's all."

Pete kissed her gently. "Thanks. You're a beaut."

Sharon had gone to bed, leaving Pete to man the radio in case a message came through, promising to let her know if anything came through. There could not have been any change during the night, she thought as she got dressed. She noticed that with Mrs. Weston absent she hadn't received her cup of tea in bed.

She ran downstairs, straight to the office. She hoped to find Pete there to ask if there was any news. She found him sitting at the radio set, fast asleep. She shook him gently.

"Pete, wake up," she said quietly.

Pete was instantly on the alert. "Oh it's you," he said sleepily. "I thought it was the radio."

"Have you been here all night?" she asked in amazement. "Have you heard anything?"

Just at that moment the radio crackled and Sharon heard Nat's voice calling Weston Downs. Her hands began to shake and her mouth felt dry. "Quick Pete," she said anxiously.

Pete didn't need any telling. He was already giving their call sign and identifying himself. "Nat, how is Mother?" he asked quickly.

"No change I'm afraid," Nat told him in a tired voice. "Steve says it might be a week before they know anything definite. Everything possible is being done to pull her through. We've just got to wait and hope. At least she hasn't had another attack. That is something to be thankful for."

"Let us know straight away, won't you? Are you staying on?" Pete asked.

"For a few days, anyway," Nat replied. "If anything crops up you can't cope with, give me a call."

Pete seemed to draw himself up. "There won't be any need for that," he said proudly.

"I know that really," Nat assured him, adding, "—er—how's Sharon?"

Pete grinned up at Sharon before answering. "She's O.K. She's here with me now if you want to talk to her."

Sharon blushed, refusing to meet Pete's eyes. His expression was bland, but she knew his brain was working overtime.

"Sharon, are you all right?" Nat's voice came through.

Sharon hadn't known what to expect, but Nat's

voice held nothing but friendliness. She felt a little disappointed until she realized he would be careful anyway with the entire Outback listening in. Therefore she kept her own voice cool and calm as she replied, "Fine thanks, and don't worry. Pete has everything under control."

"That's good. Put him on again will you. We'll talk again later," he promised with slightly more warmth in his voice.

Sharon handed the mike over, her heart beating rapidly. Dare she read anything into his last words? She indicated to Pete by sign language that she was going to make a drink, and Pete nodded his understanding.

Sharon made a pot of coffee, taking the tray through to the office, where Pete was just finishing his conversation with Nat. He looked a bit depressed as he took the cup and saucer Sharon held out to him. "It doesn't sound very good about Mother, does it?" he remarked gloomily.

"Cheer up, Pete. At least she hasn't got any worse. That must mean something," she tried to assure him.

"I suppose so," he answered, not in the least convinced really.

"I must go and freshen up," he said after finishing his coffee. "It's a good job the men know their jobs. I'm so late."

"You can't help that," Sharon said. "I'll see about some breakfast for you, then I'll carry on in here, if that's all right with you."

"Carry on as if Nat was here," Pete told her, "and let's hope nothing unexpected happens."

Two things happened, as it turned out, in that two

visitors arrived. From Sharon's point of view, one welcome and one most unwelcome. Janie arrived just before lunch, in her father's private plane. The pilot just dropped her off and took off again immediately, as he was needed in Darwin.

Pete was out on the run when she arrived, and it was left to Sharon to welcome her. She was a bit worried in case Janie thought she was one of Pete's girls, but she needn't have been. Janie was open and friendly, and the girls took to each other on sight.

Pete came in early for lunch, having seen the plane. His eyes lit up when he saw Janie. Sharon saw him open his arms wide and Janie run into them. Sharon thought it was time she disappeared, and left them to their reunion. At lunch, Pete was gay and teasing with Janie, and Janie's happiness was very apparent. On her finger was her engagement ring, and she knew that this time it was for keeps.

Sharon was thrilled for them both, then fell to wondering if she would soon feel the same. Was Nat going to tell her he loved her, or not? He had given her no real encouragement to hope, but his last kiss had told her he loved her. At least she thought it had.

Her confidence was shattered soon after lunch, when an overlanding car covered in red dust pulled up outside. A girl in a brown trouser suit, her dark hair showing from underneath a scarf, got out. Sharon went towards her with a smile.

"Hello," she said. "Can I help you?"

"You must be the office help," a high sharp voice, oddly at variance with her classical beauty, answered her rudely. "I am Miranda McMillan. Nat asked me to come and take over here. In fact I will probably be here permanently, whether Mrs. Weston lives or dies, because Nat and I will be married shortly."

Sharon's smile faded and all the colour left her face. She didn't know what to say to this hard-faced callous girl. As it happened, she wasn't expected to say anything.

Miranda pushed past her saying, "See to my luggage, then get one of the men to put the overlander away. I'll stir those lazy Abos up for some lunch myself."

Sharon was left standing on the veranda, her thoughts in a whirl. So that was Miranda! And Nat had asked her to run the homestead, and worse still, they were to be married. Even with her own terrible unhappiness, she could feel it in her heart to be sorry for Nat. Miranda would not make him happy.

She went on towards the stockyards, blinded by tears. She had been on her way to her appointment with Mitch when Miranda arrived, and saw no need to change her plans. Let her see to her own luggage, the cold unfeeling bitch, she thought. Here to stay whether Mrs. Weston lived or died, she had said. How dared she talk about that lovely woman like that.

Cold anger was gradually replacing Sharon's unhappiness. She didn't know what Nat saw in her, and didn't care. Let him marry her. He would regret it in five minutes. She felt sure Miranda must have been careful not to have let her true nature show through to Nat, or he would have told her where to go.

Nat was a hard man in some ways, as anyone with his responsibilities had to be, but underneath he was fair and compassionate, as Sharon herself had seen. He had even kissed her as if he had meant it, in order to make his mother happy, and he must have hated the deceit.

Mitch broke into her thoughts. "I didn't know whether you would come or not, ma'am, I mean Sharon. How is Mrs. Weston?"

His kindly weather-beaten face showed his concern, and Sharon impulsively took his hand. "No change, I'm afraid," she said quietly. "I'll let you know the minute we get any different news."

"That's real nice of you," Mitch told her. "Mrs. Weston has been real good to me, and the old Boss when he was alive. Nat is the same."

He seemed lost in memories for a moment, then added, "How's the little girl?"

"She is picking up nicely. Nat told Pete this morning, so he could tell her parents."

"That's good news, at least. Now then, are you ready to come and saddle Daisy?"

Daisy met them with a whinny as they reached the paddock where Mitch had put her. Sharon gave her a lump of sugar and rubbed her nose. She continued to talk to her as she saddled her, glad she hadn't forgotten how to do it.

Mitch checked everything, then told Sharon to mount up whilst he fetched his own horse. Soon they were trotting away from the homestead. Sharon put her unhappy thoughts into cold storage, to be brought out again later, and concentrated on the ride.

They rode for a long time, picking their way through the tufts of spiny spinifex with their edible oats. It seemed to be everywhere. They had to be careful also that the horses didn't get hurt falling on the stony surfaces they came across.

Mitch pointed out a herd of wild horses, brumbies he called them, telling Sharon they caught so many of them each year to be broken in as work animals. Sharon would have rather they stayed wild and free, but knew better than to say as much to Mitch. There was no room for softness in this area.

They had long lost sight of the homestead when they came to a dry river bed, overhung with an odd assortment of trees, their roots reaching deep into the earth to pick up the life-giving moisture left from the rains. The water soon drained away, to be stored underground to fee the hardy trees.

Mitch told Sharon they would rest awhile, then to her surprise he pulled a scorched tin out of his saddle pack. "Time for a smoke-oh," he grinned at Sharon's look of astonishment.

He gathered twigs together and soon a fire was burning merrily. He filled the tin with water from his canteen and dropped some tea in. A few minutes later he was pouring it into two tin cups, handing one to Sharon.

She found the milkless tea slightly bitter, but very refreshing, and leaned back against a tree, watching as Mitch rolled a cigarette between his brown calloused fingers.

"If you ride out alone, never go out of sight of the homestead like this," Mitch suddenly said. "It is easy to get lost, and you could die of thirst before you were found. Water holes are very scarce and you would be lucky if you stumbled on one."

"I am not likely to do that," Sharon assured him. "I would be too scared to go out alone."

"Better that way," Mitch told her, then sat silently smoking.

Sharon looked round her. Pete was right. The

silence could almost be heard. The bright sunshine and clear clean air accentuated the stark beauty of the landscape, its orange and red earth standing out against the brilliant blue of the cloudless sky.

Her gaze settled on some trees with pretty drooping branches. "What are those trees?" she asked.

"Wilgas," Mitch replied. "They can be used for fodder. Some areas they are grown especially for that."

"And this one?" she asked as she looked up at the branches of the tree she was sitting under. She suddenly realized it was the tree of her dreams, and she shuddered at the vivid recollection of it. Nat holding her in his arms, making love to her.

"Sorry," she said, realizing she hadn't heard Mitch's answer.

"The tree is the coolibah," Mitch repeated. "Otherwise known as the eucalyptus."

"I prefer the name coolibah," Sharon said, staring up at it again.

Mitch put the fire out and put the tin and mugs back in his saddle-packs. "Shall we start back now?" he asked. "This is far enough for your first ride."

"Oh please, not yet," Sharon begged, reluctant to have to go back to face Miranda again.

"O.K." Mitch agreed. "We'll go back the longer way. We should just make it before nightfall then. Are you sure you can manage it?"

"Of course," Sharon replied, sounding more confident than she felt, but anything was better than coping with Miranda.

They made their way along slowly, not talking much, past rocky outcrops, and sandstone boulders left in bygone days by rivers which had long since disappeared. In the distance Sharon saw herds of cattle grazing peacefully.

After all the semi-desert, she was surprised when they came upon what she termed an oasis. "This is one of the natural water holes," Mitch told her. "Most of the water we use is pumped up from underground. We have a series of artesian wells round the station, and bore holes for the stock to drink from."

Sharon's oasis was like a Paradise. The water was surrounded by a copse with all different kinds of tree. She could identify the palms and pines, and also the coolibah, and Mitch told her the others included sandalwoods and red river gums.

They stood in the shade for a while, then let the horses have a drink of the cool water, before setting out again.

The sun was setting as the homestead came into sight, and Sharon sat enthralled by it. Mitch smiled indulgently at her cries of admiration at the sight.

The sky was a mass of colour. What began as fiery shades of red and orange, with streaks of gold, gradually changed to softer colours, mauves and lilacs, pale pink and light green.

Sharon saw the sudden nightfall in this area unfold before her eyes. The beautiful colours changed again to greys and browns, then suddenly the sky was deep purple and stars began to appear.

She turned to Mitch, her face alight with pleasure. "Thank you for being so patient with me," she told him. "You must be tired of waiting."

"No ma'am," he told her sincerely. "To watch you watching the sunset was a treat for my old eyes."

Sharon blushed. It seemed strange to be getting a

compliment from this man of the Outback. The horses were getting fidgety, so they moved on and were soon back at the stockyards, where Sharon rubbed Daisy down and fed her.

"See you tomorrow, Mitch," she said when she had finished. "Thank you again."

Mitch touched his hat, smiling to himself as he returned to the task of seeing to his own horse.

Sharon felt her stomach muscles tighten as she entered the house, bracing herself to meet Miranda again. It was Pete and Janie she saw first however.

"Hi, stopout," Pete said with a smile. "I would have sent out a search party out for you by now if you hadn't been with Mitch. I knew he would bring you home safely."

Sharon forced a smile in response. "It was great fun, and Mitch stopped with me to watch the sunset."

"Beautiful isn't it?" Janie said. "I don't think I would ever grow tired of it. We're just going to call Nat. Are you coming?"

"Not now thanks," Sharon replied, surprised her voice sounded so calm. "I am going to soak my aches away. My backside is numb."

Pete and Janie went into the office still laughing, leaving Sharon to drag herself upstairs. She stiffened when she met Miranda on the landing, coming from Mrs. Weston's room.

"Where have you been?" Miranda demanded. "You are paid to do a job, not to roam about all afternoon. And why didn't you see to my luggage when I told you to. I had to get one of the Abos to do it. I am in Mrs. Weston's room, by the way," she added. "I'll move if she comes back."

Sharon suddenly felt red hot anger seering through her. Her eyes flashed fire and she found her tongue.

"In the first place, I have Nat's permission to ride in the afternoon. Secondly, I didn't see to your luggage because it isn't my job to wait on you. And finally, and most important of all, who the hell do you think you are, moving into Mrs. Weston's room? You're not Mistress here yet."

The colour suffused Miranda's face. "I soon will be," she said from between clenched teeth, "but you won't be here to see it. You are fired."

Sharon laughed in her face. "Nat hired me, and only Nat can fire me. Until such time as he does, I'll carry on."

With that she marched away, her colour high and her nerves tingling. Miranda's voice followed her. "We'll see about that. I'll talk to Nat in the morning."

Sharon ignored her, going into her room. She flopped on the bed, shaking from head to foot. She had enjoyed that, but she knew it was the end for her at Weston Downs. She would certainly lose her job when Nat returned, if not before, if Miranda had her way.

Suddenly it was all too much for her. She buried her head in the pillow and sobbed her heart out. It was much later when she crawled off the bed to get her bath. She knew she would be late for dinner, but she didn't care.

She was just brushing her hair when someone knocked at the door. Sharon called "Come in," and to her amazement Nell came in with a tray. She looked unhappy when she said, "Miss Miranda sent your dinner. Told others you too tired to come down."

So that was the way it was going to be, Sharon thought. No eating with the family. Well that suited her. At least she wouldn't have to sit with Miranda.

"Thank you Nell. I'll leave the tray outside the door. Is that all right?"

"Yes, Miss Sharon," Nell replied. "You make better boss lady than her."

Sharon smiled, pleased with Nell's open compliment. She only picked at her meal after Nell had gone, and was about to put her tray down when Nell appeared again, this time with coffee. "She don't know," she whispered, "and me not telling."

She had to laugh at Nell's mischievous expression, and they exchanged trays. Suddenly her heart felt lighter. Miranda wouldn't get all her own way with the Aborigine staff. They didn't take too kindly to Miranda's high-handed ways. They could be led, but not forced. Nell had shown that, however much Miranda might think she was in command, and respected by everyone, in reality she was disliked and made fun of behind her back.

It was the one comforting thing amongst the unhappiness and anxiety which otherwise filled Sharon's thoughts. It still didn't stop her crying herself to sleep though.

Thirteen

Next morning, the first person Sharon saw was Pete. He beckoned her into the office. Sharon was instantly alert as she hurried after him.

"What is it, Pete?" she asked urgently. "Is it your mother?"

"No, she is still the same. I called Nat a few minutes ago," he replied. "I just wanted a word with you. Janie suddenly asked me if I had known you before you came here. I bet it was that snake Miranda who said something to her. I didn't want Janie to know that we had worked it out between us to get you this job, so I'm afraid I told her I had met you before, but that you were Nat's friend, not mine."

Sharon didn't answer immediately because a sound behind her caught her attention. She turned and went to where the door was standing ajar. She looked out just in time to catch sight of Miranda disappearing into the dining-room.

Oh no, she thought. Had Miranda heard what Pete had said? If so, did it matter? For herself she didn't care. It was Pete she was concerned for. If she wanted to, Miranda could cause trouble for him, both with Nat and Janie.

Neither of them would be particularly pleased to hear Pete had brought her to his own home. But he didn't, she argued with herself. As it had turned out, Pete had only told her of the job. Mrs. Carter from the Agency had offered it to her. She heaved a sigh of relief.

"Sharon, what are you doing?" Pete's voice was impatient.

Sharon came back into the room, her face thoughtful. "Pete, do you and Miranda get on all right?" she asked.

"She hates my guts," he replied bluntly. "I've seen the nasty side of her too often, the one Nat doesn't see. She sees to that. Why?"

"Well I think she was outside the door a minute ago and heard what you said."

Pete paled under his tan. "Oh God, no," he groaned. "If she tells Janie, I will lose her. She knows about my girlfriends, but she wouldn't stand for me bringing one here. As for Nat, he'll be mad as hell. He hates lies and deceit, and he thinks you being here was a coincidence."

"But it was a coincidence, Pete," Sharon told him quietly. "I had made up my mind not to ask for the job as you suggested. I don't like anything deceitful either. Mrs. Carter at the Agency offered it to me. If she had suggested anywhere else instead, I would have gone. I didn't come here to be with you. I just wanted to see the Outback." And a bit nearer to Nat, she added to herself.

She had been watching Pete's face as she spoke. She had seen it change from despair, through amazement, to relief and joy.

"The truth is always best," he admitted. "Do your worst, Miranda, and I'll give the explanations."

Just at that moment the door burst open and Janie stood there, Her face pale and her eyes flashing angrily. So Miranda had heard, Sharon thought, and had wasted no time in stirring up trouble. She certainly was an all time bitch.

"I suppose I had to expect to see you two together, after what Miranda just told me," Janie stormed. "Well enjoy yourselves. I'm going to call my father and get him to fetch me home."

Pete strode over to her and caught her by the arms. "Janie, listen to me, please," he said quietly. "Don't believe Miranda. It just isn't true."

Janie pulled herself free. "Leave me alone, Pete. I have had enough."

Sharon thought it was time for her to intervene. "Pete is telling you the truth, Janie. We did not arrange between us for me to come here. The Agency in Darwin offered me the position."

Janie's eyes began to show a little doubt, but she still wasn't convinced. "It has got to be more than coincidence that you are here. You met Pete in Darwin," she accused.

Sharon suddenly made up her mind about something. "Yes, and I also met Nat."

"What has that got to do with it?" Janie demanded.

"Everything," Sharon replied. "Pete and I are friends, I admit that, but that wouldn't have brought me to the Outback. I came for one reason only, and that was to be near Nat. You see, I love him."

A shocked silence followed her announcement, and she saw two pairs of eyes staring at her, Pete's incredulous and Janie's full of happiness. She had known immediately that Sharon was telling the truth. It was in her voice and in her face.

She turned and went into Pete's arms, beginning to cry. "I'm sorry, Pete," she sobbed. "Please forgive me."

Pete gathered her close, and Sharon felt it was time for her to disappear. She went out of the office, closing the door softly behind her, but she doubted whether Pete and Janie would have heard if she had slammed it. They were too occupied with other things.

She was pleased Miranda's spite had done no real damage to Pete's and Janie's relationship, and she would tell her what she thought of her when they met. She went to the kitchen to make some coffee and toast, but Nell had beaten her to it.

"Just going to bring it to you," Nell said, indicating the tray. Sharon smiled her thanks, then sat down at the kitchen table to eat it. There was still no sign of Miranda when she had finished. Pete and Janie were nowhere to be seen either, so Sharon decided against going to the office in case they were still there.

Instead, she wandered out into the sunshine. She hadn't really had a good look around, so decided now was as good a time as any. She might not get many more chances, she thought unhappily. Soon she would have to leave, and the thought brought tears to her eyes.

What was life going to be like without Nat, not seeing him or hearing his voice? Her mind went back to the first evening she had met him. She had thought him hard and arrogant, and he had kissed her on the terrace.

Naturally that brought to mind the time he had made love to her at the hunting camp. Her body ached with longing as she re-lived the moments of such exquisite bliss.

She recalled her thoughts to the present with great difficulty. What was the use of torturing herself with what had been, and what could have been in the future.

She forced herself to take in her surroundings. There were the married quarters, some with washing hanging outside, drying in the sun, and the bunkhouse and cookhouse for the other ringers.

Little children played in the dirt, and women stood in small groups, breaking off their conversations to smile or call a greeting. Sharon walked past the hospital, and the store where everything from clothes to cooking pots could be bought.

She committed it all to memory, ready to be conjured up sometime in the future, somewhere else in the world. She didn't know where she was going, only that she would have to leave Australia. She would go to see Julie and Colin, tell them she didn't like it after all, then move on, perhaps to New Zealand.

By this time, Sharon had walked full circle and was back at the house. The first person she met was Miranda, her face a picture of hate. "Looking around?" she asked. "It might be the last time. As soon as Nat comes home, be ready to leave. Pete will probably be leaving too when I tell Nat what you and he did. Has Janie arranged to leave yet?"

Sharon's temper boiled over. "No, and she won't be either. Your malicious tale-telling didn't work. They are still together, and when I tell Nat the truth, they will be staying. You won't succeed in coming between Pete and Nat, I promise you."

Miranda's eyes narrowed. "Nothing you say will make the slightest difference," she said confidently. "Now get out of my way."

Sharon watched her storming off, then seeing Pete and Janie emerging from the office, decided to get on with her work. At all costs she must have the office neat and orderly before she had to leave.

Pete and Janie called a greeting as they went outside together, then Sharon set to work with a vengeance. By lunchtime it was all but finished. She fetched her lunch herself, telling Pete when he asked that she was going to carry on in the office until it was time for her to go riding.

Not even Miranda was going to stop her going for her ride with Mitch. She was determined that she would not allow Miranda to give her orders to her.

Sharon finished the clearing up in the office in plenty of time to go for her ride, and she surveyed her handiwork with pride. Not a loose paper could be seen anywhere. Apart from the ones she wasn't sure about, which she had clipped together and put in Nat's desk, they were all filed alphabetically in the correctly labelled drawers of the cabinet.

Whatever else Nat thought about her, at least he wouldn't be able to fault her work, she thought, which was some small consolation.

Whilst out riding with Mitch, during a lull in the

conversation, Sharon decided she was not going to let Miranda walk all over her for the short time she had left on Weston Downs. She would defy her orders to eat in her room, and let her do her worst. She knew if it came to a showdown, Pete and Janie would be on her side, which was a big comfort.

She could have laughed aloud at the look on Miranda's face when she went into the lounge for her pre-dinner drink. She had already told Nell what she intended to do, much to the Aborigine girl's delight.

Sharon was the last one down, and the others all had their drinks before she arrived. Pete jumped up to ask what she would like, and Janie invited her to sit by her.

Miranda's face, which had worn an astonished expression at Sharon daring to come down became blacker at the prize treatment Sharon was receiving from the others. She knew now that all three of them were against her, and her temper rose. She knew she couldn't say anything now, but looked forward to having her revenge when Nat returned. With a bit of luck, her story would rid her of all three of them at one go.

They went into dinner and the game of Miranda-baiting went on. Janie played up to Pete beautifully, emphasizing the fact that they weren't going to split up, and all three deliberately left Miranda out of the conversation.

Even Nell joined in, serving Miranda last, and that was the final straw. Miranda threw down her napkin and stormed out of the room, and didn't rejoin them afterwards.

Sharon sat with Pete and Janie in the lounge for a while after dinner, then seeing they wanted to be alone, whilst pretending they didn't, excused herself and went to the kitchen to talk to Nell and Minnie.

Instead of going home at their usual time, both girls stayed chatting, and Sharon persuaded them to have some tea with her. They asked her about England, and listened in fascinated silence to what she told them.

It was late when Sharon went up to bed, but she could still hear murmurings from the lounge, indicating Pete and Janie had no intention of following suit. She had enjoyed the evening despite everything, and it wasn't until she was lying in bed that her unhappiness surfaced with a vengeance, and once again she cried herself to sleep.

The Miranda-baiting meal wasn't destined to be repeated during the next three days. Pete and Janie were out on the run all day, taking a packed lunch with them, and Miranda had her dinner in her room, or rather Mrs. Weston's room.

Sharon's thoughts swung between Nat and Mrs. Weston. Nat called in at a prearranged time every day, and Miranda made sure she was in the office at that time. Consequently, Sharon didn't even get the chance to hear Nat's voice. Nothing would have persuaded her to be there as well.

She felt sure Miranda wouldn't say anything about her and Pete over the air. She would know that Nat would be furious to have the family's personal business broadcast for anyone to hear. No, Miranda would wait and tell him the moment he returned.

The three days following that fateful dinner dragged by for Sharon, and she became more and more unhappy. How she got through them, she didn't know. The whole atmosphere of the homestead had changed. It seemed unnaturally quiet without Nell's and Minnie's previous happy laughter and chatter. Only Miranda's voice was heard, continually shouting at them.

Without her daily ride with Mitch, Sharon felt she would have gone mad. Mitch knew something was very wrong and asked her several times what it was, but she always answered, "Nothing."

It was on the fourth day, and Sharon was feeling worse than ever when she went to meet Mitch as usual. The unhappiness, and sleepless nights, was telling on her, her spirit reaching low ebb. Mitch's kindness was her undoing, and she broke down and cried.

Bit by bit Mitch drew the truth from her about Miranda, and even about her love for Nat.

"The boss will sort her out when he comes back," Mitch assured her.

"You don't understand, Mitch," Sharon cried. "He and Miranda are going to be married soon. She told me so herself."

Mitch looked puzzled. "I must have been mistaken then," he said thoughtfully. "I could have sworn he had other ideas."

"What do you mean?" Sharon asked.

"Nothing," Mitch replied quickly. "I know one thing though. If she stays, I go, and probably others too. I hope the boss comes back quick or he won't have a crew. Her ladyship has already upset a lot of folks, I can tell you."

They looked up as a plane came into view. Mitch shaded his eyes. "Looks like the doc's plane. Wonder what he wants."

"He could be bringing little Emily home," Sharon replied.

They continued their ride and arrived back at the stockyards about an hour later. Sharon paled when she saw Nat waiting for them, his face like thunder.

"I want to talk to you, Sharon," he said sharply.

Sharon didn't want to hear. She suddenly wheeled Daisy about and galloped off, instinctively following the route she and Mitch usually took, to the dry river bed.

"Come back, you little fool," Nat cried.

Sharon looked back to see Mitch holding Nat's arm, his face grim, then she concentrated on staying in the saddle. Daisy was enjoying her gallop, her ears upright and alert.

A few minutes later, Sharon heard hoofbeats behind her, and she saw Nat coming up on her fast. The chasing horseman of her dreams, she thought, urging Daisy on to greater effort.

The river bed loomed up and Daisy suddenly stumbled in one of the wide cracks in its surface. Sharon was thrown over Daisy's head to land winded but otherwise unhurt underneath her dream tree.

Suddenly Nat was beside her, lifting her into his arms and kissing her as if he would never stop. "Oh my darling," he whispered, "I love you, I love you."

Sharon wondered if she had hit her head when she landed, and was imagining the whole thing. The chase, the coolibah tree, and Nat making love to her. Perhaps she was dreaming again.

"Sharon, speak to me," Nat said urgently.

"What about Miranda?" was the first question which sprang to mind, so she asked it.

"She will soon be gone, my darling, for good," Nat replied. "I could wring her neck for what she has been doing."

"Who told you?" Sharon asked dazedly.

"Mitch told me everything," he replied grimly.

Sharon suddenly came to her senses. "Nat, your mother, how is she?"

"She is out of danger and going to be fine if she takes it easy. She sent me back to you, telling me to marry you soon. Will you?"

"Will I what?" Sharon asked, her mind reeling.

"Marry me, of course," Nat replied tenderly. "I love you."

There were a lot of questions still to be answered, but Sharon knew now that there was going to be plenty of time. Her face radiated her happiness as her heart unfroze. "I love you too, Nat, and I will marry you, but quickly please. I can't wait."

Nat's eyes darkened with passion. "I can't wait either, my darling, and don't intend to," he said, his voice husky with emotion, and proceeded to kiss her wildly, his hands caressing her.

Sharon made one last effort before she was lost. "What if someone sees us, Nat?"

"I don't care," Nat replied thickly, and proceeded to prove it.

Sharon's happiness knew no bounds as they fulfilled their love, under the coolibah tree.

ABOUT THE AUTHOR

CHRISTINE BAKER was born in the tiny village of Harley in Shropshire, England. A few years later her family moved to her present home of Broseley. After passing the high school examination at age ten, Christine spent the next five years with her studies before taking a job as a clerk with an engineering firm. Married at age seventeen, Christine then worked as an assistant librarian until her daughter and son were born. She started writing after both children entered school.

CIRCLE OF LOVE

Step out of your world and enter the Circle of Love.

Six new CIRCLE OF LOVE romances are available every month. Here's a preview of the six newest titles on sale May 15, 1982:

#16 INNOCENT DECEPTION by Anne Neville (#21516-7 • $1.75)

It was a chance for Laurel to taste a life of unaccustomed luxury. But little did she realize the consequences of impersonating her glamorous, coldhearted twin sister—or how her own heart would betray her once she was thrust into the arms of Derek Clayton, her sister's estranged but wealthy husband.

#17 PAMELA by Mary Mackie (#21505-1 • $1.75)

Pamela woke in a hospital room with no memory of her past, no knowledge of her name. Her only thought was of her instant attraction to the hostile and handsome man before her. Pamela did not recall anything he told her of her past... and even worse, she felt herself plunging headlong into careless desire for this dangerously seductive man.

#18 SAND CASTLES by Alexandra Kirk (#21529-9 • $1.75)

Jason Kent always got what he wanted. And now he wanted Melissa to give up her independence and become governess to his young, motherless daughter. But could she cope with the desires which welled up in her heart when Jason was near? And could she stand to be so close to him—and watch him marry another woman?

#19 THE WISHING STONE by Jean Innes
(#21518-3 • $1.75)

Katie Boswell had no qualms about giving up her city life—no regrets about becoming her widowed aunt's young companion. But why must Aunt Vee insist on playing the matchmaker—calling upon the ancient powers of the Wishing Stone to make her dreams for Katie come true?

#20 THE TEMPESTUOUS AFFAIR
by Margaret Fletcher (#21501-9 • $1.75)

Their first meeting had been stormy; their second, a shock. But now Vivienne Scott stood beside Julian Garston—the father of the man she was engaged to marry—and knew she loved him. But no one else must ever know.

#21 CIRCLES OF FATE by Anne Saunders
(#21522-1 • $1.75)

Anita was confused. No, overwhelmed! She had come to Isla de Leyenda—The Island of Legend—to see Casa Esmeralda, her mother's ancestral home and to meet Edward. She should be happy, yet all she could think of was another man—a man she hardly knew!

CIRCLE OF LOVE

O

With Circle of Love Romances, you treat yourself to a romantic holiday—anytime, anywhere. Enter The Circle of Love—and travel to faraway places with romantic heroes. . . .

21502	GOLD IN HER HAIR	$1.75
21507	ROYAL WEDDING	$1.75
21500	DESIGN FOR ENCHANTMENT	$1.75
21510	THE HEATHER IS WINDBLOWN	$1.75
21508	GATES OF THE SUN	$1.75
21509	A RING AT THE READY	$1.75
21506	ASHTON'S FOLLY	$1.75
21504	THE RELUCTANT DAWN	$1.75
21503	THE CINDERELLA SEASON	$1.75